Never Kiss An Alligator On The Lips!

The Life And *Trying* Times of Boudreaux The Cajun

Volume II

Curt Boudreaux, M.Ed.

Never Kiss An Alligator On The Lips!:
The Life And Trying Times of Boudreaux The Cajun

Copyright © 1999 By Curt Boudreaux

Published by Synergy Press
Golden Meadow, Louisiana 70357

Published in the United States of America

Printed by Franklin Southland Printing
Metairie, Louisiana 70002

ISBN 1-889968-56-0

Cover design and special illustrations by Dolores Granger

Photo by Mike's Framing and Photography

CONTENTS

Chapter 4
Boudreaux On Health Care 41

DEDICATION

This book is dedicated to

Mr. Donald G. Bollinger

whose love of God, family and community

exemplifies the Cajun spirit.

He has been an inspiration to many.

I am truly grateful for his staunch support and encouragement

of me as an educator, speaker and author.

I deeply value and appreciate his friendship.

ACKNOWLEDGMENTS

Special thanks and appreciation are expressed to the following people for their contributions:

Edmund Cappel, retired educator and my former English teacher, for editing the manuscript. It was no easy task separating the good, the bad, and the ugly.

Delores Granger, a very talented and giving person, for designing the cover and creating several illustrations.

Norris Rousse, a friend who provided information on the Cajuns' migration to Louisiana and on the Boudreaux genealogy.

Juli Miller, for her wonderful endorsement. Her warmth and friendliness make television interviews fun and enjoyable.

Sue Boudreaux, Paul Champagne, Carol Miller, Ralph Miller, Della Oglesby and **Brent Vizier** for their wonderful recipes.

Harold Adams, John Amedee, Molly Blanchard, L.C. Boudreaux, Roger Bourgeois, Deacon Sammy Burregi, Karyn Buxman, Paul Champagne, Katie Collins, Martha Collins, Mike Collins, Wayne Couvillion, Jene DeCuir, Harvey Detillier, D.D.S., Nancy Gore, Shannon Guidry, Anthony Guilbeau, Sr., Glenn Kidder, D.D.S., Larry Keonig, Ph.D., Henry Lafont, Patsy Landrus, Terry Landrus, Joan Boudreaux Ledet, Monsignor Francis Legendre, Edwin Luquette, Mike Marino, Evelyn McCorkle, Vince Melvin, Donald Owen, Judy Papa, Father Edward Ramagosa, Sharyn Scheyd, John Serigny, John Simoneaux, Pastor Jim Shears, Ernest "Bob" Theriot, Barbara Thibodaux, Murray Thibodaux, Deborah O. Ventre, Lynn Vincent, Pat Vizier, and Betty Wade for their wonderful stories and anecdotes. Without their contributions this book would not have been possible.

Kelly Gaubert, and Franklin Southland Printing for putting together the final product. She is truly a joy to work with.

Testimonial

Never Kiss An Alligator On The Lips!

"Laughter is the key to good humor and a healthy soul! If you follow the life and times of Boudreaux — you'll roar with delight. **Never Kiss An Alligator On The Lips!** is a must for your daily dose of laughter! Keep it handy for reading over and over again! I promise you'll learn sumdin' new 'bout dem Cajuns every time, cher!"

Juli Miller
News Anchor-Reporter
WDSU-TV, NBC Affiliate
New Orleans, Louisiana

INTRODUCTION

Boudreaux, The Cajun, took us through some hilarious adventures in Volume I. Feedback was positive and plentiful. These stories were so well received that it is only fitting and proper to continue in that vein, hence, Volume II. People want and need to laugh, and these stories help them to achieve that. I believe I succeeded in helping people from all cultures laugh and to see the brighter side of life. And that's the intent of this book as well.

It's amazing how much interest people all over the world have in the Cajun culture. Volume I was sent to almost every state in the union and several foreign countries. They were gifts for relocated Cajuns and others who simply enjoy Cajun humor and insights. Nonetheless, it was very gratifying and rewarding to learn of its wide distribution and acceptance.

So ole Boudreaux and his podnas will take up where they left off — seeing what kind of mischief they can get into and looking at life from a different perspective — always having fun in the process, though. Fun is an essential and necessary ingredient when viewing the Cajun lifestyle.

I want to again emphasize that it is not my purpose to demean anyone. This book is simply a parody or caricature of life using Cajuns as the main characters. Any ethnic group would suffice, but as a Boudreaux, it is more appropriate for me to present the material in a Cajun context. In my opinion, Cajuns are the best people in the world and in no way would I want this book to detract from that.

The basic format of this book is very similar to Volume I, but there are a few changes. The history of the Cajuns' migration to Louisiana is repeated for the benefit of those who do not have the first book. This short section provides interesting and valuable background information about the Cajuns. As an added bonus, a brief Boudreaux genealogy is presented for those who may have a special interest in knowing more about the history of this family. Hopefully, this will prove to be meaningful and might even prompt some Boudreaux's to pursue it further and delve into their past.

At the beginning of each chapter, there are some "You just might be a Cajun if..." statements as well as "Some words you will probably never hear a Cajun say....." These should provide an amusing insight into the Cajun mindset.

And of course the "meat" of the book once again is the Boudreaux stories. An abundance of them has been received from many and varies sources just waiting for you to indulge yourself. Remember to turn to the glossary when you run into an unfamiliar word as you are reading these stories. Or, if you're not Cajun, you may want to begin by reading the glossary first in order to prepare yourself.

Since Cajuns love to cook and eat, the Lagniappe section contains a few mouth-watering recipes for your culinary pleasure. So get the black pot out, turn on the burner, and get ready, sha!

Enough said! It's time to kick back, relax, and with your favorite beverage in hand shout, "Laissez Le Bon Temps Rouler!"

Chapter 1

In The Beginning

In the spring of 1605, the French established a colony in Nova Scotia called Port-Royal.   It was the first European settlement in North America, preceding Jamestown by two years and the landing at Plymouth by fifteen.

In 1671, a census revealed sixty-seven families at Port-Royal. The list was ladened with family names very similar to a modern day telephone directory in south Louisiana.   From Aucoin to Daigle to Pitre to Thibodeaux.

The ownership of Acadian country changed hands a number of times during the succeeding years.   England and France were in a constant state of war, with short periods of peace between conflicts.   But the colony hung on and prospered in spite of this. By 1750, some families were entering their third generation of colonization.

The Treaty of Utrecht, signed in 1713, awarded Acadia's 2,500 inhabitants once again to England.   The Acadians were informed that they would be required to swear an oath of allegiance to England in order to stay.   They tried to have the wording changed but to no avail.   Their basic concern was that in the continuing battle between England and France, they might be forced to bear arms against their Mother country.   They protested for forty years.

But one day a British commander, acting without specific orders, took historic steps to clear the colonists from the land.   He sent armed soldiers and ships to Nova Scotia with instructions to burn the villages.   The order instituted one of the most talked about displacements in history.

It was a time of terror. Of more than 18,000 Acadians in that fateful autumn of 1755, over half disappeared forever. For those who survived, there was no more home for them in the land of their ancestors. They had no more country. They embarked for the unknown, without a backward glance, fleeing forever. Uprooted and hopeless, it was said that "all they had left was their hands and their prayers."

Each of the British colonies was forced to take some of the Acadians. None were forewarned of this except Massachusetts and Connecticut. They were unwelcomed guests since no provisions were made for their support.

Some were immediately rejected by their host governments and encouraged to return to Nova Scotia or France. Otherwise, they could fend for themselves in the British colonies. Some were even indentured in Georgia and the Carolinas. Many were permanently separated from their families.

Between 1764 and 1767, hundreds of Acadians immigrated to Louisiana. Arriving from Santo Domingo, Maryland and New York, these first Acadians were followed by many others. Their arrival in the colony marked the final stage of a tragic odyssey which had begun in Acadia and lasted for nearly a decade.

The long years of exile had neither broken their spirit nor undermined their ethnic unity. The circumstances of their early history had molded their character and thinking, so that now in Louisiana they were determined to preserve and continue their philosophy and way of life.

They were a fun-loving people with an unusual fondness for music, dancing, and above all, their beloved balls. On horseback, on foot, and by pirogue, they traveled as much as thirty to forty miles to attend these dances. At the sound of a couple of fiddles, young and old alike danced to their heart's content, usually well into the night.

Just as popular as the balls, but by far more practical, was the widely practiced custom of the boucherie. Taking turns to provide the animal to be slaughtered, neighbors and friends gathered for the day to cut and prepare the meats which were later divided among the participants. The original intent was to furnish people who did not have refrigeration with meat for immediate consumption, but in time the boucherie became a social occasion. It provided people with the opportunity to visit, exchange news and maintain contact.

Acadians were a close knit people. Their lives revolved around the family unit and the home. Families gathered during the evening to review daily activities, discuss the weather, crops and especially to reminisce. The Acadians were excellent storytellers and well versed in their rich history and folklore. They repeatedly related tales of their beloved Acadia, keeping the past alive for their children and grandchildren. These early Louisiana Acadians jealously guarded their religious and ethnic inheritance and left an indelible cultural pattern for many generations to come.

The word "Cajun" evolved from the Acadians themselves. They pronounced the word Acadian in French as "A ca jan" which eventually was shortened to "Ca jan." As the years passed, more and more people simply began saying "Cajun" as it is used today. It is often said in Cajun country that there are two groups of people in the world: Cajuns and those who want to be. Which group are you in, sha?

Chapter 2

Boudreaux Genealogy

Like other surnames of Acadian origin that rank among the ten most frequent in Louisiana, that of Boudreaux occurs throughout the southern part of the state. A few Boudreauxs were among the earliest Acadian immigrants to come to Louisiana in the 1760's, but most of the Boudreaux's arrived in 1785 in the large migration from France.

The many Boudreaux families living in Acadie before the expulsion all descended from Michel Boudrot, a native of the LaRochelle area in west-central France. He arrived in Acadie about 1642 with his wife, Michelle Aucoin. By 1686, Michel had become a "Lieutenant-general" of the king at Port Royal. His several sons spread throughout Acadie, some staying in Port Royal, others settling in Pisiquit, Beaubassin, and Grand Pre. After the expulsion, Boudreaux families were exiled to various points along the Atlantic seaboard, to England, and to France.

By 1766, at least three Boudreaux families were living in Louisiana. Two had settled along the Mississippi River in what is now St. James Parish. One of these families was headed by Oliver Boudreau, the great grandson of the original Cajun settler, Michel. The second family was headed by Joseph Boudreau, about whom we know very little. The third family, led by Jean Boudrau, also a great grandson of Michel, came to the Attakapas with his wife, Marguerite Guilbau, and their son, Jean Charles Boudrau.

Jean Boudrau and his family probably arrived in Louisiana in 1765 with the Acadian contingent led by Joseph (Beausoseil) Broussard. Through his only son, Jean-Charles, (who was married in 1785 to Dorothee Comeau), Jean began an important line of Boudreaux's in the Attakapas area.

First settling along the upper Vermilion River near what is now Lafayette by the 1860's, the descendants of Jean-Charles had spread as small farmers southward into the Cote Gelee area near today's Youngsville, and some had moved along the lower Vermilion in the vicinity of Abbeville.

Another early Boudreaux settler in the Teche area was Augustin-Remy Boudreau, who came to Louisiana as an orphan at the age of thirteen with one of the Breaux families from Maryland. By 1777, Augustin-Remy had joined the local militia in the Attakapas and about five years later married Judith Martin and settled in the Bayou Bourbeaux area near Grand Coteau. Most of Augustin-Remy's descendants remained in the Grand Coteau area for much of the 19th century, but by the 1860's, some had moved to the Church Point area.

Other lines of Boudreauxs in the Attakapas area were established by Acadian refugees from France who arrived in Louisiana in 1785. Among these were Joseph Boudrau, who was married in 1792 to Elisabeth Trahan and who obtained land on Bayou Vermilion near Lafayette. Their three sons and many of their offspring remained in the area for some time, but by the mid-19th century most had migrated into the northern part of Vermilion Parish.

Oliver Boudreaux's was the first Boudreaux family to settle on the Acadian Coast along the Mississippi River. He was a widower who arrived in Louisiana from Acadie with his son, Simon Boudrau, probably in 1765. Oliver remarried in 1767 to Anne Gaudet, and they settled on a farm on the west bank of the Mississippi River in St. James Parish. Their son, Simon, married Monique Dupuis in 1774. He became a respected planter in the St. James area and, and by the time of his death in 1824, owned a four hundred acre plantation below Donaldsonville. Simon Boudreaux, Jr. continued in his father's footsteps as an antebellum planter.

Several Boudreaux families who came with the Acadian group from France in 1785 also settled along the Mississippi River, many at St. Gabriel below Baton Rouge and in Ascension Parish. Among these were Francois-Xavier Boudreaux, his wife Marguerite Dugas, and his widowed mother Bridgette Apart, who had been married to Antoine Boudreau. Francois-Xavier had two sons: Etienne Boudreau who moved to the Lafourche area, and Joseph Boudreaux who moved to Opelousas.

In 1785, eighteen Boudreaux families arrived in New Orleans with the sixteen hundred Acadian exiles from France. Some of these were sent to settle along the Acadian Coast, but most of them settled along Bayou Lafourche where each family was given land, animals and tools. Many of those who first settled on the Acadian Coast also moved to the Lafourche area shortly after their arrival in Louisiana. By the beginning of the 19th century, many Boudreauxs had begun to migrate southward toward the Gulf, most making homes near present-day Thibodaux, others moving deeper into Terrebonne Parish. By 1850, Lafourche and Terrebonne Parishes contained nearly half of the state's Boudreaux households.

You just might be a Cajun if.....

You consider the seasons of the year to be Winter, Spring, Summer and Hunting.

Your boat has a higher appraised value than your house.

Some words you'll probably never hear a Cajun say.....

"Tank God faw geem wardens!"

"Ah ain't puttin' no dawg in da back o' my pickup truck, me."

Chapter 3

Boudreaux On Animals

Sweet Revenge

There was a big party on the bayou hosted by the richest man in South Louisiana. He had recently built a huge tank and stocked it with many alligators, paranas and other man-eating reptiles. To liven up the party, he issued a challenge to all of his guests. He announced that if anyone was brave enough to swim the length of the tank he would gladly grant them three wishes. Not surprisingly, there were no takers. So the party continued with everyone "passing a good time."

Suddenly, there was a huge splash. As the host looked on, he could see a man swimming like crazy across the tank with the reptiles chopping at his heels. The crowd was cheering wildly! Lo and behold, the man made it unharmed across the tank. As he climbed out, it became obvious to everyone that the brave soul was none other than ole Boudreaux.

The host excitedly ran up to him, grabbed his hand and offered his sincere congratulations. "Wow, Boudreaux," said the host, "You made it! What a courageous thing to do! So what are your three wishes?"

"Well, da furst ting ah want, me, is a double barrel shotgun," said Boudreaux.

"No problem," said the host.

"Da sacand ting is two shells faw da shotgun," replied Boudreaux.

"Done," responded the host.

"And da tird ting ah want, me, is faw ya ta sho me da son-of-ba-gun dat push me in dat tank!" shouted Boudreaux with fire in his eyes.

Timely Names

Boudreaux stopped to visit Shawee and couldn't help but notice his two new dogs.

"Man, das some nice lookin' dogs ya got dere," commented Boudreaux. "Wat's dere neems?"

"Timex and Rolex," replied Shawee.

"How come ya neem dem someting so stoopid like dat?" questioned Boudreaux.

"Maaaaay, cuz dey some watch dogs, dem!" replied Shawee.

Spoiled By Success

Boudreaux had a great hunting dog named Priest. He was by far the best on the bayou. One of Boudreaux's friends, Bubba, from North Louisiana came for a visit and accompanied him on their annual duck hunting trip. Bubba was amazed at how good Priest was and couldn't stop singing his praises.

When Bubba returned the following year, he noticed immediately that Priest was no where in sight. Boudreaux actually had another dog at his side ready for the hunt.

"Priest wuz da bestess huntin' dog ah aver seen, me. Dere wuz none mo bedda den him," commented Bubba. "May ware's he at, Boudreaux?"

"He's dead, sha," replied Boudreaux. "Ah hadta shoot'em."

"You shot Priest!" exclaimed a shocked Bubba. "May how come?"

"Well," explained Boudreaux, "He wuz so good dat ah kinna felt like ah hadta give'm a promotion. So ah chenged his neem from Priest ta Monsignor. And arry since ah done dat, he don't wanna do nuttin' but lay aroun' all day long and sit on his behind!"

Enough Said

Boudreaux was walking down the street on his way to work and saw a parrot in a pet store. He stopped for a moment to admire the bird.

The parrot looked at him and said, "Hey man, you are REALLY ugly!"

Boudreaux was furious and stormed past the store heading for work.

On the way home he saw the same parrot in the window. Seeing him, the parrot looked Boudreaux squarely in the eyes and said, "Hey man, you are REALLY ugly!"

Boudreaux was fit to be tied. His anger turned into rage as he marched into the store to confront the owner.

"Look!" shouted Boudreaux. "Dat dum bird ya got dere in da winda done called me ugly two times, him! Ya don't git'm straight ah kin tellya rat na, ahm goin' sue da pants offa ya, kill dat bird breen and use'm faw crab bait!"

"I'm so sorry, sir," replied the owner trying to get Boudreaux to calm down. "I can assure you it won't happen again."

Just to be sure, Boudreaux passed by the store on his way to work the next morning. The parrot looked at him and said, "Hey, man,"

"Wat?" asked Boudreaux.

The parrot winked and said, "You know!"

Rough Rider

Boudreaux decided to try his hand at horseback riding although he had no prior experience or training. He mounted the horse and steadied himself in the saddle. As the horse reached a full gallop, Boudreaux slipped from the saddle. He grabbed for the mane but was unsuccessful. He tried to throw his arms around the horse's neck but that failed, too. In a last ditch effort to save himself, he frantically jumped from the horse in an effort to hurl himself to safety, but unfortunately his foot got caught in the stirrup. He was now at the mercy of the horse's pounding hooves. His head struck the ground again and again and again, mere moments away from unconsciousness, when....... the Wal-Mart manager ran out to turn the horse off!

In High Demand

Shawee was sitting on his front porch and saw a funeral procession coming up the street. As it got closer, he saw a hearse followed by a second hearse and, oddly enough, Boudreaux walking behind them. Also walking in the procession behind Boudreaux were some two hundred men.

"May Boudreaux, who's in dat furst hearse, dere?" asked Shawee.

"Dat's my wife, Chlotilde," replied Boudreaux.

"Chlotilde? May cot dawg, wat happened?" inquired Shawee.

"My dawg, Phideaux, he bit hur and she died," said Boudreaux.

"Dat's a sheem, yeah," said Shawee sympathetically. "Well den who's in dat sacand hearse, dere?"

"Aw dat's jis my mud-'n-law," responded Boudreaux.

"Caaaaaw, wat happened ta hur?" questioned Shawee.

"May Phideaux bit hur, too, and she didn't make it edda," explained Boudreaux.

Shawee reflected for a moment then asked, "Sha lawd! You don't tink ah could rent dat dawg from ya faw a lil while, do ya?"

"Haw yeah!" answered Boudreaux. "Butchu goin' havta stan' in line, you. Watchu tink dem two hundred mans, dere, is followin' dis procession faw?"

The Real Thing

Boudreaux and Gaston went to the New Orleans airport to pick up Shawee. He was returning from a trip to Mexico. As they waited for him to come out of the jetway, everyone deplaning was talking about how great Cancun was. They were singing its praises with things like "Cancun was fantastic", "Cancun was terrific", and "Cancun is the best"!

"Ya kno wat, Gaston," said Boudreaux. "We could make us a forchune, us."

"May watchu meen?" asked Gaston.

"Cuz arrybody gittin' off da pleen, dere, is talkin' bot how good dat can coon is," explained Boudreaux. "Jis tink wat dey would pay us faw da fresh coon!"

Just Following Instructions

Chlotilde returned from Delchamps and placed several bags of groceries on the kitchen table. Boudreaux peeked in one of the bags and pulled out a box of animal crackers. Opening the box, he spread them on the table and began carefully looking through them. "Wat in da world you doing, you?" asked Chlotilde. "Maaaaay, da box say dat ya can't eat'em if da seal is broken. So me, dere, ahm lookin' faw da seal!" explained Boudreaux.

It's Grrrrrreat

One morning Boudreaux called his friend T-Brud and asked, "Kin ya pleez come ova ta da house ta hep me? Ah got me dis big jigsaw puzzle, dere, and ah can't figa out how ta git dat ting started."

"Ahm good, good at dat, me," answered T-Brud. "You sho axed da rat guy, you. By da way, Boudreaux, wat's da puzzle abot?"

"Well, from da pitcha on da box, it look lika tiger," said Boudreaux.

"Ahma come ova rat away!" said T-Brud

Boudreaux let him in and took him to the kitchen where the puzzle was spread out on the table. T-Brud studied the pieces of the puzzle very intently, then he picked up the box and examined it very carefully.

"Da furst ting," said T-Brud, "No matta wat ah do me, ah ain't goin' be able ta sho ya how ta assemble dis ta look like da pitcha o' dat tiger."

"Aaaaaw, dat's a sheem," said Boudreaux.

"Da sacand ting, dere," continued T-Brud, "Ah tink ya oughta git yosef a cup o' coffee and den put all dese Frosted Flakes back in da box!"

Too Doggone Strong

Boudreaux went to the store to buy some detergent. The clerk asked if he had a lot of clothes to wash.

Boudreaux answered, "Oh non, it's not clothes ah gotta wash, me. It's my dawg, Phideaux."

"Then be extremely careful," warned the clerk. "This detergent is very strong and could make your dog sick or even kill him."

Boudreaux decided to keep it anyway and went home. One week later he returned to the store to buy a six-pack of Bud.

The clerk was curious to find out how things had turned out, so he asked, "How's your dog?"

"Phideaux? May he died, him," replied Boudreaux.

"I warned you about that detergent," said the clerk. "I told you it was too strong to use on a dog!"

"Aw non," said Boudreaux, "Ah don't tink it wuz da detergent, me. Ah tink it wuz da spin cycle."

Ragin' Cajun

A baby crawfish and its mother were walking along a ditch when the baby crawfish, who had gone ahead, came scurrying back down the ditch.

The mother crawfish asked, "What's the matter?"

"Look at that big thing right there!" answered the baby.

"Oh don't worry about that," answered the mother crawfish confidently. "That's just a cow. It won't hurt you."

They continued walking. Within minutes the baby crawfish came running back a second time. The mother again asked, "What's the matter?"

"Look at that big thing over there!" replied the baby.

"Oh don't worry about that," said the mother with assurance. "That's just a dog and it won't do you any harm."

They continued walking. Moments later the baby crawfish came rushing back a third time.

"What's the matter?" asked the mother crawfish.

"Look at that big thing over there!" said the baby fearfully.

The mother's eyes got bigger and bigger and in a split second she took off running.

"What's wrong, mother?" cried the baby crawfish.

"Run for your life, son!" said the mother crawfish looking back. "That's ole Boudreaux, the Cajun, and Cajuns eat anything!"

Speak Now Or .....

"Oh Boudreaux, you got da parrot dat ah sentcha faw ya birtday?" asked Shawee.

"Haw yeah," said Boudreaux, "and it wuz good, good, too!"

"You don't mean ta tell me datchu ate dat bird?" asked Shawee in a state of shock.

"May yeah," answered Boudreaux.

"Couyon, dat bird could talk five different languages, him!" exclaimed Shawee.

"Huh, den he shoulda sed someting!" replied Boudreaux.

Mixed Breed

Boudreaux and Gaston were sitting on his front porch. Boudreaux was holding his new puppy. It was a strange looking little rascal. It had the face of a beagle, the body of a "weenie" dog, and the hair of a poodle.

Gaston couldn't resist any longer so he asked, "May wat kinna mut you call dat, you?"

"Datsa somma dawg," said Boudreaux.

"A somma dawg?" questioned Gaston. "Ah ain't nava heard o' dat, me."

"Ah yeah," responded Boudreaux, "It's somma dis and somma dat!"

Big Ears

Boudreaux bought a mule and when he tried to get it in his barn, its ears hit the top of the door. He pulled the mule back, got his saw off the wall and was ready to cut the top of the barn door. But his "podna", Gaston, was passing by and saw what he was doing.

"May why don'tcha jis take yo shovel, dere, and dig a lil slant hole at da door?" suggested Gaston. "Dat way you ain't goin' havta cut ya door."

"Couyon! It's not his legs das too long, non, it's his ears!" exclaimed Boudreaux.

Eggstra Sized

Boudreaux and Shawee were sitting on the front porch swing admiring his chickens.

"Das sho some nice lookin' hens you got dere, Boudreaux," commented Shawee.

"Haw yeah!" replied Boudreaux, "And dey lay some big, big eggs, too!"

"Aw non!" said Shawee.

"Das rat. In fac, dey so big dat it only take eight o' dem ta make a dozen!" explained Boudreaux.

Sacrificial Lamb

Boudreaux and Shawee were walking near the edge of the woods. As they were talking, Boudreaux suddenly grabbed Shawee by the arm pulling him back.

"Cot dawg, Shawee!" said Boudreaux. "You gotta be mo' careful, you. Looka dat big hole you almos step in, dere!"

Shawee looked down in the hole and commented, "Sha lawd, dat sho look lika deep hole, yeah. Ah wunda, me, how deep it go?"

To satisfy their curiosity, they found a rock, threw it in, and listened to see how long it would take to hit the bottom. They didn't hear anything. They found a bigger rock and repeated the process, but still didn't hear it hit. Shawee noticed a railroad tie lying in the bushes. He picked it up and threw it into the hole.

While they were listening for the railroad tie to hit the bottom, a little billy goat came charging out of the bushes. It ran right between them and jumped into the hole. A few minutes later their "podna", Cowan, came walking through the bushes.

"May, Cowan, watchu doin' way out here in da woods, you?" asked Boudreaux.

"Ahm jis out here lookin' faw my lil billy goat," answered Cowan.

"You ain't goin' bleeve dis, non, Cowan," said Boudreaux. "Da streengist ting done jis happened here. A lil billy goat jis came runnin' lika bat outa hell from dem bushes, dere, and jumped rat in dis deep hole!"

"May dat couldna been my billy goat," explained Cowan. "Cuz my lil goat, him, wuz tied ta a railroad tie back dere in doze bushes."

Finish The Job

Boudreaux and Kymon wanted to go hunting but didn't have a place to hunt.

"Dere's dis ole farma down da road das a fran o' mine," said Kymon. "He's old, him, and can't even git out in da fields no mo'. Ah betcha he'd lettus hunt dere, yeah."

Upon arrival, Kymon told Boudreaux that he would go into the house and ask for permission to hunt on the farmer's land. Kymon went into the house, and his friend, the old farmer said, "Das okay wit me, yeah, Ky, but could ah gitcha ta do a lil fava faw me, dere?"

"Haaaaaw yeah, anyting you axe," responded Kymon.

The farmer said, "My ole huntin' dawg, Snake Eyes, he's sooooo old, him. He's all da time in peen. Ah need ta put'm outa his misery but ah jis don't got da heart, me. Befo' you go in my field, dere, couldja pleez use yo gun and do it faw me? He's in da front yard and in a lota peen. He can't even make it inta da house no mo', him."

Kymon told the old farmer that he would help him and started out of the house to tell Boudreaux that they would be able to hunt there. As he was walking down the front steps, he thought of an idea for a joke to really scare Boudreaux.

"Did he say dat we could hunt on his land?" asked Boudreaux.

As a joke, Kymon said, "NO! Dat ole son-a-ba-gun! Das da most meanest ole man ah done aver seen, me! Ahm goin' show'm someting!"

Kymon aimed his gun at the dog and shot. "Das goin' teach'm a lesson he ain't nava goin' fogit!" shouted Kymon.

Boudreaux quickly ran into the farmer's barn and Kymon fell on the ground with laughter. He had scared Boudreaux enough to cause him to run away and hide.

Suddenly, Kymon heard —BAM....BAM! Boudreaux raced out of the barn and yelled to Kymon, "Okay, ah got da hoss and da cow, me! We betta git outa here in a hurry, na!"

I've Got My Pride

The Acadiana Zoo was bringing a large female gorilla to the Audubon Zoo in New Orleans. Just outside of Thibodaux, the gorilla began to go berzerk, making it difficult to drive the transport truck. The zookeepers realized that the gorilla was in heat and pulled off the road to try to determine what to do to calm her down.

One of the zookeepers suggested that they find someone to mate with the gorilla to keep her calm until they could get to New Orleans. About this time, ole Boudreaux came walking down the street toward the truck.

"Hey mister," said the zookeeper to Boudreaux, "I've got a proposition for you. How about $100.00 to mate with that gorilla in the back of our truck?"

Boudreaux scratched his head and thought about the offer for a minute.

"Okay," said Boudreaux reluctantly, "Ahma do it but only on teree conditions, dere."

"Fine. What are they?" asked the zookeeper.

"Well, da furst ting," started Boudreaux, "Nobody kin watch cuz, ta tellya da troot, it's kinna embarrassin'!"

"No problem," replied the zookeeper.

"Da sacand ting is," continued Boudreaux, "You can't tell my mama nuttin' abot dis, non. She's a good Catlic, hur. She go ta church arry Sunday, and it would kill hur ta fine out someting like dis."

"Done," said the zookeeper. "Now what about the third condition?"

"Ah hate ta axe ya dis," said Boudreaux, "Butcha tink dis could wait til Friday cuz das wen ah git paid, me?"

Bird Brain

Boudreaux had to appear in court for a hunting violation. As he approached the bench, the judge said, "Boudreaux, you've been charged with shooting and killing a bald eagle. Is that correct?"

"Das rat, yo hona," replied Boudreaux.

"Don't you understand what the bald eagle symbolizes for this country and how it's protected and valued?" questioned the judge.

"Haaaaaw yeah, ah sho do, me," answered Boudreaux.

"Then why in the world would you shoot such an American treasure? And then have the nerve to make a gumbo?" continued the judge.

"May ah tought it wuz a duck, me," said Boudreaux.

"Well, your penalty will be a $2000 fine and six months in jail," said the judge sternly. "By the way, tell me, what did it taste like?"

"Uuuuuh, kinna lika cross between a brown palican and a whooping creen," responded Boudreaux.

Pure Thoroughbred

Boudreaux took his "podna", Shawee, to see the psychiatrist. "You gotta hep my fran here, dock," said Boudreaux. "He tink he's a hoss, him."

"Why do you say that?" asked the doctor.

"Cuz he walk aroun' on all fours some o' da time, he graze in da grasses, and den he whinnies jis lika hoss do," explained Boudreaux.

35

"Well, I've handled cases like this before so I know I can help him," said the psychiatrist, "But I have to tell you up front that it's going to be extremely expensive."

"Money ain't goin' be no prablum dere, dock," replied Boudreaux, "Cuz he done alrady won two races, him!"

Teaching A Lesson

Boudreaux and Chlotilde were at the zoo on a warm, spring day. Chlotilde was wearing a cute, loose-fitting, pink spring dress. It was sleeveless with straps. They walked through the ape exhibit and passed in front of a cage with a very large gorilla. As they did, the gorilla "goes ape." He jumped up on the bars, holding on with one hand, grunting and pounding his chest with the free hand. He was obviously excited at the sight of Chlotilde.

Boudreaux noticed this excitement and said to Chlotilde, "Oh beb, les have a lil fun, us, wit dat gorilla, dere. How bot you tease dat big ape a lil bit, huh? Go hed and pucka ya lips, wiggle yo behin' jis a lil bit, dere, and play along wit him."

Chlotilde reluctantly followed Boudreaux's suggestion. The gorilla became even more excited and began making noises that would wake the dead.

Then Boudreaux said, "How bot you let one o' dem straps, dere, on ya dress fall down."

She did and the gorilla was just about to tear the bars down.

"Na try pulling ya dress up ta ya tighs," coaxed Boudreaux.

This drove the gorilla absolutely crazy.

Without warning, Boudreaux quickly grabbed Chlotilde by the hair, ripped open the door to the cage, and hurled her in with the gorilla. Boudreaux looked at her and said, "Na, go hed and tell HIM you got a hedache, beb!"

Concerned Citizen

Boudreaux called the parish council office to express a concern and to make a request.

Said Boudreaux, "Hey Cap, ah wanchall ta move dat deer crossin' sign on our road, dere."

"What's the reason for your request?" asked the administrative officer.

"Cuz alota dem deers, dere, is gittin' hit by caws so ah don't want dem ta cross dere no mo'." explained Boudreaux.

Specially Trained

Boudreaux had a Labrador retriever since it was a pup and trained him to be used during duck season. He sold him for a handsome price to his "podna", Shawee. After several hunts, Shawee came to complain to Boudreaux.

"Oh Boudreaux," said Shawee, "Ah want my money back, me, faw dis dawg."

"May how come?" asked Boudreaux.

"Cuz he ain't no good, him, das how come," explained Shawee. "He din git one duck yet!"

"Maybe ya jis not tarowing him high enuff!" responded Boudreaux.

Dangerous Doggy

Upon entering the little bait shop on the bayou, the stranger noticed a sign saying, "Danger! Beware of Dog!" posted on the glass door. Inside, he noticed a harmless old hound dog asleep on the floor beside the cash register. He asked the worker, Boudreaux, "Is that the dog folks are supposed to beware of?"

"Haaaaaw yeah, das him!" replied Boudreaux.

The stranger couldn't help but be amused. "That certainly doesn't look like a dangerous dog to me," he said. "Why in the world would you post that sign?"

"Cuz befo' ah put up dat sign, dere," explained Boudreaux, "Arrybody jis kept trippin' all ova him."

Mule Headed

Boudreaux had a part-time job working at the funeral home. As he went to work one Monday morning, he discovered a dead mule in the yard. He called the police. Since there did not appear to be any foul play, the police referred Boudreaux to the Health Department.

They said since there was no health threat that he should call the Sanitation Department. The supervisor there said he couldn't pick up the mule without authorization from the mayor.

Boudreaux knew the mayor and was not eager to call him. The mayor had a strong temper and was generally hard to deal with, but Boudreaux called him anyway.

The mayor did not disappoint him. He immediately began to rant and rave at Boudreaux and finally said, "Why did you call me anyway, Boudreaux? Isn't it your job to bury the dead?"

"Haw yeah, it's my job ta barry da dead alrat," said Boudreaux. "But ah always like ta notify da next o' kin furst!"

Rare Footwear

Boudreaux went to the shoe store in the mall to buy a pair of alligator shoes. He walked in, found a pair he liked and tried them on.

"Ahma take dese," said Boudreaux. "How much dey cos?"

"The price of this particular pair is $500.00," replied the clerk.

"Cot dawg, das high, yeah!" exclaimed Boudreaux. "Ah can't afford dat, me, but ah sho want a pare o' some alligata shoes bad, bad."

"Then perhaps you ought to go out and kill an alligator and take care of it yourself," suggested the clerk.

Boudreaux thought about it and decided that it was a good idea. So he headed for the swamp to get an alligator. Some three hours later, Shawee passed by in his pirogue. He saw at least ten dead gators stacked one on top of the other.   He also saw Boudreaux shoot another one.

"Wat in da world ya doin', Boudreaux?" asked Shawee. "You los yo mind, you?"

"Ah wanna git me some alligata shoes," answered Boudreaux. He picked up the gator he had just shot, turned it over and said with disappointment, "Doggone Shawee, dis one ain't got no shoes on needa!"

You just might be a Cajun if.....

You make the sign of the cross when you pass by Floyd's Record Shop in Ville Platte.

You think the Fab Four are Doug Kershaw, Wayne Toups, Clifton Chenier, and Rocking Doopsie.

Some words you'll probably never hear a Cajun say.....

"Sha, ah can't eat some o' dem crawfish, non, cuz my cholestrol's too high."

"Ah ain't goin' eat no sacand helpin', me, cuz ahm puttin' on too much weight."

Chapter 4

Boudreaux On Health Care

The Right Prescription

Boudreaux wasn't feeling well, so he decided to call his doctor. "Hey, dock," said Boudreaux, "It's been a munt since ah went ta see ya and ah still don't feel no bedda, non."

"Well, are you following the instructions on the bottle of medicine I gave you?" asked the doctor.

"Haw, yeah," said Boudreaux, "It say rat dere on da bottle, 'keep tightly closed', so dat wat ah been doing, me!"

False Positive

Boudreaux wasn't feeling well so he went to his doctor for a check-up. After a thorough examination and numerous tests, the doctor gave him the bad news. He had cancer and only six months to live. Boudreaux shared this information with everyone he saw. He and his son, Junya, were at Wal-Mart and ran into Shawee.

"Shawee, da dockta tol me dat ah got aids and only got six munts ta live," said Boudreaux soberly.

"Dat's a sheem, Boudreaux," commented Shawee. "Ah feel bad, bad, me."

They talked for a while longer and Shawee moved on to continue his shopping.

"Oh Poppa," asked a puzzled Junya, "How come ya tol arrybody else, dere, dat you wuz dying o' cancer, but ya tol Shawee dat ya got aids?"

"Cuz ya kno Shawee, dat big macrow, him," explained Boudreaux, "If ahda tol him dat ah wuz dying o' cancer, he'd be here hangin' aroun' ya mama tamorra."

Moment of Truth

Chlotilde and some of her friends left early one Sunday morning to go to a bowling tournament in New Orleans. Boudreaux received a telephone call around 7:00 PM that evening from one of Chlotilde's companions informing him that she was in the hospital. They brought her to the emergency room because she had had a severe allergic reaction to something she had eaten. The caller suggested that Boudreaux come quickly. So without hesitation, he jumped in his car and drove the thirty miles to the hospital hoping that all would be well when he arrived.

Upon arriving at the hospital, Boudreaux was delighted to see that much of the swelling and redness had gone away and the allergy appeared to be under control. After Chlotilde explained to Boudreaux what had happened, Maree, one of her friends said, "Oh Boudreaux, ya not gonna bleeve wat da dockta axed Choltilde!"

"May wat?" inquired Boudreaux.

"He wanna kno, him, if she wuz sexually active!" blurted Maree. "Das someting, yeah!"

"Huh, me, dere, ah jis wanna kno wat hur ansa wuz! Cuz if she say yeah, ah wanna kno wit who, me!" exclaimed Boudreaux.

Strange Sounds

Boudreaux woke up one morning and couldn't hear out of his right ear. This was not totally unexpected since he was eighty-six years old, but he decided to have his doctor check it anyway.

After a thorough examination, his doctor said, "Boudreaux, I've got some good news for you. You're not losing your hearing. You've got a suppository stuck in your ear that's clogging it up!"

"Chooooo! Dat's some good news, yeah!" said a jubilant Boudreaux.

"Good news? Why do you say that?" asked the doctor.

"Cuz na ah kno ware da earphone faw my radio is!" replied Boudreaux.

Just To Be Sure

Boudreaux's unwed niece was very tearful and distraught as she came to visit him and Chlotilde.

"Wat's da matta, sha?" asked a concerned Boudreaux. "How come ya cryin' like dat?"

"Nonk Boudreaux," said his niece, "Ah jis found out, me, dat ahm pragnant an ahm scaid ta tell poppa and mama. Dey goin' be so hurt, dem."

"Hol on, beb," advised Boudreaux. "Don't give up so easy. Monday mornin', dere, me and you goin' go down ta da dockta's office and git one o' dem DNA tesses done ta fine out if it's really yors!"

The End Is Near

Boudreaux was very distraught when he called his doctor.

"Oh dock," said Boudreaux, "Ah wanna kno abot dat medicine you gave me, dere! You tolme dat ah gotta take it faw da rast o' my life?"

"Why yes, Boudreaux, I did," answered the doctor.

"Den ahm jis wundring, me, how come ya didn't tell me how serious my condition is!" exclaimed Boudreaux.

"What do you mean?" asked the doctor.

"Cuz it say rat dere on da bottle, 'NO REFILLS'," responded Boudreaux excitedly.

Still Going Strong

Boudreaux went to his doctor for a checkup. After running numerous tests, the doctor said, "You know, Boudreaux, you're in excellent condition for a fifty-nine year old man."

"May, did ah say ah wuz fifty-nine, me?" asked Boudreaux.

"You mean you're not?" responded the doctor.

"Haw non. Ahm saventy-nine, me!" said Boudreaux proudly.

"Good heavens!" exclaimed the doctor. "You're in incredible shape! Let me ask you this. How old was your father when he died?"

"Did ah say my fadda wuz daid?" asked Boudreaux.

"You don't mean he's alive?" asked the doctor.

"May yeah!" replied Boudreaux. "He's ninety-eight, him, and still kickin'!"

"Wow, you must have some really good genes!" commented the doctor. "Well, let me ask you this. How old was your grandfather when he died?"

"Did ah say my pawpaw wuz daid, him?" questioned Boudreaux.

"You don't mean he's still alive, too?" said the doctor excitedly.

"You got dat rat, dock!" said Boudreaux. "Him, dere, he's a hundred and twanny-five. Annnnd not only dat, he's gittin' married next Sadday!"

"Getting married!" said the doctor in disbelief. "Why in the world would a hundred and twenty-five year old man want to get married?"

"Did ah say he WANTED ta git married, him?" asked Boudreaux.

Changing Anatomy

Boudreaux received a call at work from the hospital informing him that Chlotilde had been rushed to the emergency room. He was asked to come over immediately.

Upon arriving, he went straight to her and asked frantically, "May wat's da matta, beb?"

"Aw, ah shot mysef in da right knee, dere," answered Chlotilde.

"Shot yosef in da knee? May how could a ting like dat happen?" questioned Boudreaux.

"Ah jis been so deprassed, me, dat ah wanted ta end my life. So ah decided ta shoot mysef in da heart," explained Chlotilde. "Ah called da dockta and axed him zackly ware my heart wuz located. He tolme dat it wuz rat unda my right breast. Den ah eemed da gun rat dere and ah shot, me!"

Easy Diagnosis

Kymon stopped by Boudreaux's house one day for a visit and took the opportunity to complain a little. Said Kymon, "You kno, Boudreaux, ah tink dere's someting wrong wit me, yeah."

"How come you say dat?" asked Boudreaux.

"Cuz arrywares ah touch my body wit my finga, ah feel some peen," replied Kymon.

"Ah kin tellya rat off da bat watcha prablum is, me," said Boudreaux.

"May wat?" inquired a startled Kymon.

"You jis gotcha sef a broken finga, dat's all!" laughed Boudreaux.

Fully Loaded

Boudreaux returned from hunting one day and emptied his pockets on the kitchen table. He didn't know that his two-year old son, Junya, was watching at a distance. Boudreaux left the kitchen and went to the bathroom. Junya was attracted to those shiny things on the kitchen table and grabbed one. Before he could be stopped, he put it in his mouth and swallowed. Boudreaux picked him up quickly and rushed him to the doctor.

"Oh dock, Junya here done swallowed a tirty-eight caliba bullit," explained Boudreaux excitedly. "Wat kin ya do?"

"Well," said the doctor, "Just let him drink this laxative and take him home. We'll have to let nature take its course."

"Annyting ah should do in da meentime, dere?" asked Boudreaux.

"Yes! For God's sake don't point him at anybody!" cautioned the doctor.

Ironing Is Tough

"Oh Boudreaux, how come ya got yo leg in a cass, dere?" asked T-Brud.

"Maaaaay, ah fell offa da ironin' boad, me, and ah broke it," explained Boudreaux.

"Watchu wuz doin' on top da ironin' boad?" questioned T-Brud.

"Maaaaay, Chlotilde wudn't here so ah wuz tryin' ta iron my pants," answered Boudreaux

Light Attraction

Deep in the heart of bayou country, Boudreaux's wife, Chlotilde, went into labor in the middle of the night. The doctor was called out to assist in the delivery. Since there was no electricity, he handed the father-to-be, Boudreaux, a lantern.

The doctor said, "Here, you hold this high so I can see what I'm doing."

Soon, a baby boy was brought into the world.

"Hold on there," said the doctor. "Don't be in such a rush to put the lantern down. I think there's yet another one to come."

Sure enough, within minutes he had delivered a baby girl.

"No, no!" shouted the doctor. "Don't be in a great hurry to put down that lantern. It seems there's yet another one to come."

Sure enough, within minutes he had delivered another baby girl.

"Whoa!" said the doctor. "Hold that lantern still. I think there's another one coming!"

Boudreaux scratched his head in bewilderment and asked the doctor, "Oh dock, you don't tink dat maybe it's da light das attractin' 'em, huh?"

Sure Cure

After having their eighth child, Boudreaux and Chlotilde decided that that was enough. So Boudreaux went to Doctor Fontenot and explained his situation.

"Dock, me and Chlotilde, dere, we got us eight chiren," said Boudreaux. "Sha lawd, das enuff faw anny man ta try ta provide faw all dere needs, yeah. Wat kin we do ta not have anny mo'?"

"Well, there's a procedure called a vasectomy that could fix the problem," replied Doctor Fontenot.

"May how dat work, dat?" inquired Boudreaux.

"Go home, get a cherry bomb and light the fuse," explained Dr. Fontenot. "Put the cherry bomb in a can and hold the can up to your ear. Then count to ten."

"Oh dock, ah ain't no rocket scientist, me," said Boudreaux. "But ah sho' don't see how puttin' a charry bomb in a can next ta my ear, dere, is goin' stop me and da wife from havin' anny mo' chiren."

Boudreaux was skeptical to say the least. So he and Chlotilde drove to Texas to get a second opinion.

The Texas doctor was just about to tell them about the procedure for a vasectomy when he realized who he was dealing with. So the doctor said, "Mr. Boudreaux, this is what you do. Go home and get a cherry bomb. Light the fuse and place it in a tin can. Then hold the can next to your ear and count to ten."

Boudreaux was still doubtful and confused, but he figured both doctors couldn't be wrong. When they got home, Boudreaux got a cherry bomb, lit the fuse and put it in a can. He then held the can next to his ear and began counting on his fingers, "one...two...three...four...five..." at which point he paused, placed the can between his legs, and continued counting with the fingers on the other hand.

Good Advice

Boudreaux and Cowan were at the Hubba Hubba having a few beers. Boudreaux noticed that, from time to time, Shawee had a painful look on his face.

"May wat's dat matta witchu, Cowan?" asked Boudreaux. "How come arry na and den you got dat gremas on yo face, you?"

"Ah fell on the banket, da sidewalk ya kno, on da side o' my house dere, and arry time ah move my arm like dis it hurt me bad, bad," explained Shawee.

"Den don't move it dat way, couyon!" advised Boudreaux.

Too Close For Comfort

T-Boy stopped by Boudreaux's house for a cup of coffee. They began catching up on the day's news with their daily dose of caffeine.

"Oh Boudreaux," said T-Boy, "You aver went ta da dockta, you, faw dem peens in yo legs?"

"Haw yeah," replied Boudreaux. "Ah went las week, me."

"May wat he tolju?" asked T-Boy.

"Aw, he sed dat my veens is too close tagetta, dem," responded Boudreaux.

"Too close tagetta? May watcha mean by dat?" questioned a puzzled T-Boy.

"Ah don't kno, me. He jis tolme dat ah got varry close veens," explained Boudreaux.

The Cause Of The Problem

Boudreaux was suffering from a severe nervous condition and decided to get a checkup by the family doctor. He was accompanied by his nagging wife, Chlotilde, to Dr. Fontenot's office.

After a thorough examination, Dr. Fontenot checked his notes, nodded and wrote a prescription for a powerful tranquilizer.

"How offen ah gotta take dese pill, dere, dock?" asked Boudreaux.

"Let's start off with once every six hours. But they're not for you," replied Dr. Fontenot. "They're for Chlotilde!"

No Easy Task

Boudreaux went to see Dr. Fontenot with an unusual request.

"Oh dock," said Boudreaux, "Ah wancha ta give me one o' dem sperm tesses, dere."

"But Boudreaux, you're eighty-five years old!" exclaimed Dr. Fontenot. "Why in the world would you want a sperm test?"

"Nava you mind, you," cautioned Boudreaux. "Jis gimme dat tes!"

Dr. Fontenot decided to play along with him and said, "Okay, here's a specimen bottle. Go home and bring it back to me when you are able to provide a sample."

Boudreaux took the bottle and left the office. One week later he returned and handed an empty bottle to the doctor.

"Ahm sorry, dock," said Boudreaux, "It jis din work out. Ah tried wit my lef hand, me, and nuttin'. Den ah try wit my rat hand. Still nuttin'. Chlotilde, her, she try wit her lef hand— nuttin'. And den wit her rat hand. Nuttin'. No matta how hard we try, us, we jis couldn't git dat cap off da bottle!"

Foolproof Method

Boudreaux and Shawee were solving the world's problems at the Hubba Hubba. The more beer they consumed, the more personal the conversation became.

"You kno wat, Shawee?" said Boudreaux.

"May non, wat?" asked Shawee.

"We live in a crazy world, yeah, us," replied Boudreaux.

"How come you say dat, you?" inquired Shawee.

"Cuz my daughta, Colinda, hur, she went ta da dockta faw some birt control pill," said Boudreaux.

"May wat's so crazy bot dat?" asked Shawee as he chug-a-lugged the remainder of his beer.

"Da dockta, him, he gave hur two asprin," answered Boudreaux.

"Two asprin? May faw wat?" asked a confused Shawee.

"He say faw hur ta take one o' dem wit a glass o' wata and da udda one ta put batween hur knees and hol it dere!" explained Boudreaux.

Paying The Price

A woman walked up to a little old man rocking in a chair on his front porch. It was none other than ole Boudreaux himself.

"I couldn't help noticing how happy you look," remarked the lady. "What's your secret for a long, happy life?"

"Well, sha, ah smoke me teree pack o' cigaritts a day," replied Boudreaux. "And ah drink two cases o' Budweiser arry week, ah eat alota fatty, fatty foods, and ah don't naver axacise."

"Wow! That's amazing," the woman said. "How old are you?"

"May, ahm twanny-six, me," answered Boudreaux.

All Heart

Boudreaux and Chlotilde were shown into the dentist's office, where Boudreaux made it clear he was in a big hurry.

"No fancy stuff, dock," he ordered. "None o' dat gas or dem needle or anny kind o' dat peenkiller stuff. Jis pull da toot out and git it ova wit."

"I wish I had more patients who were as composed and poised as you," said the dentist admiringly. "Now, which tooth is it?"

Boudreaux turned to Chlotilde and said, "Go ahed, beb, show'm ya toot."

Semi-Helpful

Boudreaux went for an office visit with Dr. Fontenot who began questioning him immediately.

"What seems to be the problem, Boudreaux?" asked Dr. Fontenot. "Aren't you feeling well?"

"Aw yeah, ah feel good, good me," answered Boudreaux.

"Then why are you here?" questioned the Doctor.

"Dock, ah wancha ta gimme a hafa perscription o' dat viagra stuff, dere," said Boudreaux.

"Viagra! Good God, Boudreaux, you're eighty years old!" said the Doctor. "And besides, why in the world would you want only half a prescription?"

"Huh, so ah kin stop peeing in my shoes, me!" explained Boudreaux.

Quality Care

Boudreaux and T-Brud were drinking beer at the Hubba Hubba. In spite of the liquid refreshment, Boudreaux looked frustrated and quite annoyed.

"May wat's da matta witchu, Boudreaux?" asked T-Brud. "You look like you mad at da world, you?"

"Aaaaaw, it's my doggone healt insurance," replied Boudreaux. "Da cumpny jis chenged carriers and ya gotta decide which plan you want wit dem."

"May wat's da big deal abot dat?" questioned T-Brud.

"Sha lawd, dey got da PPO, da HMO, da ESP, da CPA and alota udda ones!" said a frustrated Boudreaux. "It look like if it ain't got teree lettas in it, dey can't cova ya."

"How you gon make up ya mind, you?" inquired T-Brud.

"Da only good ting is dat da cumpny done give us some guideline ta go by ta hep us decide," said Boudreaux. "Dis is it rat here."

Top 10 Ways You Know You've Joined A Cheap HMO

10. Da annual breast axam is held at Hooters.

9. Directions ta ya dockta's office include, "Taka lef wen ya enta da traila pawk."

8. Da tongue deprassors got da taste o' fudgesicles.

7. Da only proctologist in da plan is 'Gus' from Roto-Rooter.

6. Da only item listed unda Prevantive Care coverage is "an apple a day".

5. Ya "Primary Care Physician" is waring da pants ya gave ta Goodwill las munt.

4. Da "patient is responsible faw two hundred pacent o' outa network charges" ain't no typo.

3. Da only axpense covered one hundred pacent is embalming.

2. Wit ya las HMO, yo Prozac didn't come in different colors wit lil "m's" on'em.

And da numba one sign dat you jurned a cheap HMO.....

1. You axe faw viagra and ya git a popsicle stick and some duck tape.

"Well, Boudreaux, dat oughta be a big hep ta ya," said T-Brud. "It kinna lay arryting out faw ya, dere. It sho sound lika good deal, yeah. Ahd take it, me."

"Das wat ah wuz tinking, too," replied Boudreaux. "Ah guess ah jis wanted me a sacand opinion. Hey, Cap, coupla mo' Buds ova here fas, fas, huh?"

The Perfect Donor

Boudreaux needed a heart transplant and discussed his options with the doctor.

The doctor said, "Ah have some good news, Boudreaux. We have three possible donors. The first is a young, healthy athlete who died in an automobile accident, the second is a middle-aged businessman who never drank or smoked and died flying his private jet. The third is an attorney who died after practicing law for thirty years. Which one do you want?"

Without skipping a heartbeat Boudreaux replied, "Ahma take da lawya's heart, me, dock."

"Why would you choose that one?" asked the doctor.

"Cuz ah want one, me, dat ain't nava been used befo'!" replied Boudreaux.

Second Opinion

Boudreaux injured his leg at the camp one weekend getting out of his pirogue. By the time he got home on Sunday, his leg was very swollen, and he was having difficulty walking. He called Dr. Fontenot at his home, and he instructed Boudreaux to soak it in hot water. He tried soaking it in hot water as the doctor suggested, but the swelling only worsened and became more painful.

Chlotilde saw him limping and said, "Ah don't kno, me, ahm only da wife, but ah all da time tought it wuz mo betta ta use da cold wata, not da hot one, faw swellin'."

Boudreaux switched to cold water and the swelling immediately went down.

On Monday morning Boudreaux called Dr. Fontenot to complain.

"Hey dock, wat kinna dockta you are you, annyhow?" asked Boudreaux. "Ya tolme ta soak my laig in hot wata and it got worsa. My wife, Chlotilde, dere, tolme ta use cold wata and it got betta rat away."

"Really?" said Dr. Fontenot. "I don't understand it. My wife said hot water!"

Useful Training

Boudreaux showed up late for work one morning. He was immediately questioned by his supervisor.

"Why are you late, Boudreaux?" asked his boss.

"Ta tellya da troot, it wuz bad, bad," said Boudreaux. "Ah wuz walking down Bayou Drive and dere wuz dis tarrible wreck. A man wuz laying in da middle o' da street cuz he wuz tarown from his caw."

"Then what?" asked his boss.

"Sha lawd, his laig wuz broken, him, his skull dere wuz frachured and dere wuz blood arrywares," explained Boudreaux. "Tank God ah took dat furst aid course, me. All my treenin' came back ta me in a sacand."

"What did you do?" questioned his boss.

"Maaaaay, ah sat mysef down and put my haid batween my knees ta keep me from feentin'!" responded Boudreaux.

You just might be a Cajun if.....

You think "Dam Yankees" is a play about a cracker from North Louisiana.

You think "Baywatch" is an environmental group.

Some words you'll probably never hear a Cajun say.....

"Ah ain't goin' bring no beer on dis fishin' trip, non."

"Ahm goin' give up drinkin' beer faw Lent, me."

Chapter 5

Boudreaux At The Hubba Hubba

Works Every time

Boudreaux and Cowan were sipping a few suds at the Hubba Hubba when Cowan noticed that Boudreaux kept licking his lips.

"How come you keep lickin' yo lips, you ?" asked Cowan.

"Cuz dey chapped bad, bad, bad, dem," replied Boudreaux.

"Bestess ting faw dat," said Cowan, "Is to fine yosef a hoss, raise the tail and kiss it ware da sun don't shine."

"Dat goin' cure my chapped lips?" questioned Boudreaux.

"Haw non!" responded Cowan. "But it sho goin' stop ya from lickin'em!"

What You Don't Know Can Hurt You

Boudreaux and Shawee were indulging in a few cold ones at the Hubba Hubba and lamenting about married life.

"It's so important ta fine da right woman," commented Shawee, "Cuz das a long time, yeah, forever."

"Ah kno," responded Boudreaux. "But ah married Miss Right, me. Ah jis din kno dat hur furst neem wuz 'Always'!"

The Wrong Reason

Boudreaux and Cowan were lifting a few cold ones at the Hubba Hubba one evening.

"You kno wat, Boudreaux," said Cowan.

"No! Wat?" asked Boudreaux.

"You sho are a good husband, yeah, you," answered Cowan.

"How come ya say dat?" asked Boudreaux as he took a swig of beer.

"Cuz you take Chlotilde witchu arrywares you go!" replied Cowan.

"Being a good husband ain't got nuttin' ta do wit it," said Boudreaux.

"May watchu meen?" questioned Cowan.

"Ah jis figa dat if ah take hur wit me all da time den ah ain't gotta kiss hur goodbye!" smiled Boudreaux as he glanced toward Chlotilde.

Dirty Cover

Boudreaux and Shawee were walking home late one January night after boozing it up at the Hubba Hubba. Shawee decided to take a short cut through the cemetery, but Boudreaux was scared so he chose to stay on the main road.

Because Shawee's vision and coordination were greatly impaired on this dark night, he slipped and fell into a freshly dug grave. It had been raining, and the sides were slippery, preventing him from climbing out. He was terrified and began shouting, "Somebody, pleez hep me! It's cold, cold down here!"

Boudreaux was passing the corner of the cemetery and thought he heard a voice. He cautiously stopped and listened. There it was again, loud and clear. "Somebody out dere, pleez hep me!" said the voice. "It's cold, cold down here!"

Boudreaux reluctantly walked up to the grave, peeked over the side and said, "May, couyon! No wunda you cold, you. You dun kick all da dirt offa ya!"

In The Driver's Seat

Boudreaux and Shawee spent most of the night "getting chockayed" at the Hubba Hubba. During the wee hours of the morning, they staggered out of the establishment, scarcely able to stand up. They got into a huge car, both barely able to see above the dashboard. As they were cruising along, they came to an intersection. The traffic light was red, but they just went straight through.

Shawee, sitting in the passenger seat, thought to himself, "Ah mus be mo' drunka den ah tought, me. Ah coulda swore, dere, dat we jis pass tarew a red light, us."

After a few more minutes, they came to another intersection. The light was red and again they went through it.

Shawee was getting concerned thinking he might be losing it. He suddenly got very nervous. He decided to pay close attention to the road and was anxious to get to the next intersection to discover what was going on. Sure enough, the light was definitely red and they sped through it.

"Cot dawg, Boudreaux!" exclaimed Shawee. "Don'tcha kno datchu jis ran teree red light in a row! You tryin' ta git us killed or someting, you!"

"Sha lawd!" replied a shocked Boudreaux. "You mean AHM driving?"

Nobody's Fool

Boudreaux was out most of the night at the Hubba Hubba, drinking with his "podnas." Chlotilde awakened him early to go to work. He was very groggy as he sat on the side of the bed, putting on his shoes.

"Oh Boudreaux!" shouted Chlotilde, "You got dat drunk las nite, you? You got yo shoes on da wrong feet!"

"Don't try ta fool me, beb," answered Boudreaux. "Ah kno das my own feet, yeah!"

Hard To Find

Sipping a cold Bud at the Hubba Hubba, Gaston asked Boudreaux, "May, wares da Anglish Channel at?"

"Ah don't kno, me," answered Boudreaux. "All ah kno is dat ah can't ketch it on my talavision at hume."

Before It Hits The Fan

Boudreaux had been running his crab traps all day. From dawn until dusk, he worked his traps in the hot summer sun without catching a thing. Hot and frustrated, he stopped at the Hubba Hubba to cool off.

"Hey Cap," said Boudreaux to the bartender, "Gimme six long-neck Dixie beers dere quick, quick!"

The bartender hurriedly filled the order. Boudreaux cracked them open one at a time, and in about three minutes consumed all of them.

"Cot dawg, Boudreaux!" exclaimed the bartender. "Wat's da matta witchu? How come you drinkin' dem beers so fas, you?"

"Well, podna, you'd drink fas, too, if you had in yo pocket wat ah got in mine," said Boudreaux.

"May watchu got in yo pocket dat would make you drink fas like dat?" asked the bartender.

"Only fifty sants!" replied Boudreaux.

Fastest Thing In The World

Boudreaux and some of his "podnas," Shawee, Kymon, and Cowan were drinking beer at the Hubba Hubba. As usual, they were in deep conversation, attempting to solve the mysteries of life.

"Watchall tink is da mos fassest ting in da world?" asked Boudreaux.

"Me, dere, ah tink da fassest ting in da world is a tought," offered Shawee. "Befo' you kin tink a tought, you done already tunk it."

"Aw non, Shawee, ah kin tink o' someting mo fasser den dat, me!" said Kymon. "Ah tink da mos fassest ting in da world is da blink o' da eye. Befo' you kin tink, you done already blunk."

"Ah tink yall all wrong, me," chimed Cowan. "Da mos fassest ting in da world, dere, is da light switch. Sha lawd, you jis flip dat switch on and befo' you kin blink, dat light come on."

"Well, yall kno how much ah hate ta tell yall dis butchall all wrong, yeah!" said Boudreaux as he sipped his beer. Da mos fassest ting in da world, dere, is dockarhea. One time ah had dat dockarhea, and all of a sudden befo' ah could tink, blink or flip dat light switch, ah done messed in my pants, me!"

Tricky Fish

Boudreaux and Gaston were at the Hubba Hubba lifting, a few cold ones.

"Watchu been up to, Gaston?" asked Boudreaux.

"Aw, not too much. But me and da missus, dere, went ta one o' dem real fancy restrunts in New Orleans," shared Gaston. "Chooooo, dey had some good, good food dere, yeah!"

"May watcha ordered?" inquired Boudreaux.

"Da house specialty," replied Gaston. "It wuz some grilled tuna."

"Ahm jis wundring, me, how dey keep it from falling tarew da grill wen dey dump it outa da can?" asked a puzzled Boudreaux.

Remotely Trouble

Boudreaux and Gaston were having a few cold brews at the Hubba Hubba. As always the conversation moved from one topic to another, usually all meaningless.

Finally Gaston was prompted to ask, "Oh Boudreaux, yall watch alota talavision atcha house, yall?"

"Aw non," answered Boudreaux. "Watching da talavision meens fightin', violence and all kinna foul language, dere... and das jis decidin' who goin' git ta hold da ramote control!"

Joined At The Hip

Boudreaux and Kymon were downing a few cold ones at the Hubba Hubba. Kymon was moved to ask, "Oh Boudreaux, how Chlotilde's doin' on dat diet she went on, dere?"

"Huh, not too good, non," replied Boudreaux. "She ain't hardly loss nuttin', hur. But ah tol hur, me, da olda you git da tuffa it is ta lose weight cuz by den ya body and ya fat done got ta be real good frans and dey don't wanna part!"

Happy As A Lark

Boudreaux and Shawee were having a few cold ones at the Hubba Hubba. The conversation drifted to some of their friends.

"Oh Boudreaux," said Shawee, "Ya aver notice, you, how happy Cowan is all da time?"

"Ah kno," replied Boudreaux. "He's jis as happy as if he had breens, him!"

Who To Believe

Boudreaux and Kymon ordered another couple of beers at the Hubba Hubba.

Said Kymon, "You kno, Boudreaux, ah been tinkin', me."

"Aaaaaw lawd, dat ain't goin' be nuttin' but trouble. Ah kin tell, me," said Boudreaux as he reached for his beer.

"How come if somebody tellya dat dey got a billion stars in da universe, dere, you goin' bleeve'em, but if dey tellya a wall got wet peent on it you goin' havta touch it ta be sho?" asked Kymon.

"Ah-don't-kno me, Kymon," said Boudreaux in disgust. "Jis drank yo beer and try not ta tink so much, huh?"

No Medium Necessary

Boudreaux and Cowan were slamming a few cold ones down at the Hubba Hubba. It didn't take very long for the conversation to become philosophical.

"Oh Boudreaux," said Cowan, "If ya could have a conversation dere, a talk, wit annybody, livin' or daid, who would it be?"

Without hesitation Boudreaux replied, "Maaaaay, da livin' one!"

Back To The Basics

Boudreaux, Shawee and Cowan were at the Hubba Hubba having a few cold beers one night when they decided to get in on the weekly raffle. They bought five, one-dollar tickets each, since the money was going to charity. The following week the winning tickets were drawn and they each won a prize.

Shawee won the first prize, a whole year's supply of gumbo prepared by an award winning chef.

Cowan won the second prize, a six month's supply of boudin and hoghead cheese.

Boudreaux won the sixth prize, a toilet brush.

When they met at the Hubba Hubba a week later, Boudreaux asked the others how they were enjoying their prizes.

"Good, good!" said Shawee, "Ah could eat some gumbo arryday, me."

"Couldn't be mo' betta, sha!" replied Cowan. "Dat boudin and hoghead cheese, dere, are my two mos bestess. And how's da toilet brush, Boudreaux?"

"Not so hot, dere," confided Boudreaux. "Ah tink ahm gon havta go back ta da paper, yeah!"

A Different Approach

Boudreaux and Shawee were drinking beer at the Hubba Hubba one night, and the conversation soon turned to a personal topic.

"Ah don't kno wat else ta do, me," shared Shawee. "Wenaver ah go hume afta me and you been drinkin', dere, ah turn off da hedlites befo' ah git ta da driveway, shut off da caw engine and coast inta da garage. Ah even take off my shoes befo' ah go in da house and den sneak up da stairs. Ah git undressed in da battrum witout puttin' on da lite and den crawl real easy inta bed. Afta all dis, my wife, hur, she still wake up and yell at me faw stayin' out so late."

"May ya doin' dat all wrong, you," said Boudreaux confidently.
"Watchu mean?" asked Shawee.

61

"Me dere, ah screech inta da driveway honkin' da horn, slam da door, storm up da stairs, and tarow my shoes in da closet. Den ah jump in bed, pat Chlotilde on da behin' and say real loud, "How bot we make some luv, beb! She don't nava wake up, hur!"

Committed To The Game

Boudreaux and Cowan were indulging in their favorite pasttime at the Hubba Hubba.

"Hey Cowan, ah got me dis lil riddle faw ya, dere," said Boudreaux.

"Aw, ah like riddles, me, go hed," replied Cowan.

"Watchu call it, dere, if ya find you and Shawee in a closet?" asked Boudreaux.

"Huh, ah don't kno but it don't sound good, non," replied Cowan.

"Da winnas in las year's hide and seek contest!" laughed Boudreaux.

Who To Believe

You just might be a Cajun if.....

Your favorite talk show hosts are Okra Winfrey and Bryant Gumbo.

Your favorite band has an accordion player and fiddler, but no guitarist.

Some words you'll probably
never hear a Cajun say.....

"Ah tink dis fish is too small ta keep, yeah. Ahma tarow'm back in."

"Ah all da time folla da speed limit, me."

Chapter 6

Boudreaux On The Law

A Lesson Learned

Boudreaux and Gaston were returning home from a New Orleans Saints football game and were stopped by a police officer as they were leaving the city.

"Wat's da prablum, dere, Cap?" asked Boudreaux.

"Well, you didn't come to a complete stop at the last intersection, and there's a stop sign there," answered the officer.

"Yabbut, ah slowed down, me," said Boudreaux.

"But slowing down isn't stopping," countered the officer.

"Aw, dere ain't no difference batween da two. Dey da seem ting, dem," answered Boudreaux trying to avoid a ticket.

"No, they're not," replied the officer, "And I'll show you."

At this point the officer began pounding Boudreaux in the head with a billy club. After smacking him for about thirty seconds the officer asked, "Now, do you want me to slow down, or do you want me to stop?"

A Silver Lining

"I have some good news and some bad news," the defense attorney told his client, Boudreaux.

"Go hed and gimme da bad news furst, sha," said Boudreaux.

"Well, the bad news is that your blood test revealed that your DNA is an exact match with that found at the crime scene," said the lawyer. "It looks really bad."

"Cot dawg!" exclaimed Boudreaux. "May wat could be da good news?"

"Your cholesterol is down!" said his attorney.

History Repeats Itself

Boudreaux was in training to become a state trooper. The training was hard and rigorous but he gave his all to make it through the academy. This paid off handsomely because he passed the field part of the evaluation with flying colors. His confidence was soaring when he entered the room to take the written exam, the final hurdle. Boudreaux was devastated to learn that he didn't pass.

The training officer sympathized with Boudreaux because he knew how hard he had worked and the sacrifices he had made. Said the officer, "Boudreaux, because you worked so hard and you want this so bad, I'm going to give you another chance."

"Oh tank ya, sir!" said Boudreaux. "Ah sho preciate dat, me."

"Tomorrow I want you to tell us who killed Abraham Lincoln," said the officer.

As Boudreaux walked into the house, Chlotilde asked, "How's it goin', beb?"

"Ah must be doin' purty good, me," answered Boudreaux. "Dey alreddy done put me on a big murda case, dere!"

Lost and Found

Boudreaux went to a local car dealer to buy a new vehicle. He found one that he liked and wanted to test drive it. He swung onto the highway and started at a modest pace. From fifty miles an hour he accelerated to sixty, then seventy, eighty and finally ninety MPH. Then he heard the siren of a police car and saw the flashing lights in his rear view mirror. This prompted him to go even faster, and he suddenly found himself engaged in a high speed chase with the police. After a short time, the policeman was able to cut him off and bring him to a stop.

"What's the matter with you, mister? Didn't you see my lights flashing and hear the siren?" questioned the frustrated officer.

"Haw yeah, ah sho did, me!" responded Boudreaux.

"Then why didn't you pull over?" asked the officer.

"Well, ta tellya da troot," explained Boudreaux, "Teree days ago, dere, my wife, Chlotilde, ran away wit a cop and ah tought you wuz bringin' her back ta me!"

ESP

Boudreaux and Cowan were going home from the Hubba Hubba late one evening. Cowan, the driver, was exceeding the speed limit which attracted the attention of a state trooper. The trooper pulled them over, asked to see Cowan's driver's liscense and inquired, "Where you fellas been?"

Because of the brews he had comsumed, Cowan was "feeling his oats" and responded, "Maaaaay, ah don't see wares dat's any o' yo bidness, sha."

This prompted the trooper to hit Cowan in the head several times with his billy club. Without saying a word, he leaned over and smacked Boudreaux in the head with the club a few times, too.

"Cot dawg!" shouted Boudreaux as he rubbed his head. "How come ya dun dat, you. Ah din do nuttin, me!"

"I know how you Cajuns are, especially you, Boudreaux," answered the trooper. "Yall wouldn't have gotten fifty yards from here when you would've said, 'Ah wish heeda hit me like dat!"

Government Service

Boudreaux placed a call to the FBI office.

"Hallo, is dis da FBI, dere? inquired Boudreaux.

"Yes it is, sir. How can we help you?" asked the agent.

"Uhhhh, ahm callin' ta report my neighba, dere, Kymon," said Boudreaux. "Ah jis wanchall ta kno dat he's hidin' some marijuana in his firewood."

"This will be investigated immediately," replied the agent in a very official voice. "Thank you for the information."

The next day seven FBI agents arrived at Kymon's house. They made a thorough search of the shed where he kept the firewood, broke every log into small pieces, and were unable to locate any marijuana. They were very upset when they left.

That night Boudreaux dialed Kymon's telephone number. "Hey, Kymon. Did da FBI come ova ta ya house taday, dem?" asked Boudreaux.

"Haw yeah, saven o' dem came!" answered Kymon.

"Did dey chop ya firewood?" asked Boudreaux.

"Aw, yeah, dey sho did," responded Kymon.

"Okay," said Boudreaux, "Na it's ya turn ta call. Ah need my garden plowed, me!"

Stand By Your Man

Boudreaux and Chlotilde were returning home late one Saturday night after the fais-do-do. A policeman pulled him over and asked to see his driver's license.

"Mr. Boudreaux," said the policeman, "Do you realize you were speeding?"

"Haaaaaw non!" exclaimed Boudreaux emphatically. "Not me!"

"I'm afraid you were, sir," continued the policeman. "The speed limit here in Golden Meadow is thirty and you were doing seventy-five miles an hour."

"No way, sha," shouted Boudreaux, "And ah got me a witness ta prove it, too"

"Who?" asked the officer.

"My wife, dere, Chlotilde," answered Boudreaux. "She's rat here in da caw wit me. Go hed an axe hur!"

The officer went around the car to the passenger side and motioned to her to roll down the window.

"Mrs. Boudreaux, was Mr. Boudreaux speeding?" questioned the policeman.

"Aw ah don't kno, me, beb," responded Chlotilde. "Ah don't nava pay attantion ta him wen he's drinkin' like dat!"

The Best of Both Worlds

Boudreaux received a telegram from the sheriff's office which said, "We regret to inform you that we found your mother-in-law's body floating in the lake behind Golden Meadow with a crab on each finger and toe. Please wire instructions."
Boudreaux quickly wired back, "Sell da crabs, reset da bait!"

Conscience Check

There was a time when Boudreaux was having trouble sleeping at night. He thought he knew what was causing the problem, so late one night he began writing a letter.
"Dear Infernal Ravenue Service,
Faw da tax year 1995, ah undapaid my faderal income taxes, me, and ah ain't been able ta sleep good aver since. In dis anvelop, dere, you gonna find a check faw two hundred dolla.

Yors in good govment,
Boudreaux

P.S. If ah don't sleep mo betta tanite, ahm goin' sand ya da rast tamorra.

More Bang For Your Buck

Boudreaux was stopped by a state trooper for speeding. As the officer was writing out the ticket, Boudreaux asked how much it was going to cost him.
The officer replied, "The fine for going seventy in a fifty-five MPH zone is one hundred dollars."
"Den tell me dis," said Boudreaux. "Wat would da fine be if ah wuz goin' ninety?"
"The fine, sir, is one hundred dollars for any speed higher than fifteen miles over the limit," explained the trooper.
"Den ahm goin' be back, yeah," said Boudreaux as he drove off, "Cuz ah sho wanna git my money's wert, me!"

Gotcha!

Boudreaux and a woman were involved in a terrible car accident. Both of their cars were totally demolished, but, amazingly, neither of them was hurt.

After they crawled out of their cars, the woman said, "Wow, just look at our cars! What a mess! There's nothing left, but fortunately we're not hurt. This must be a sign from God that we should be friends and live together in peace and harmony for the rest of our days."

"Ah tink ya rat, yeah, sha," replied Boudreaux. "Dis gotta be a sign from da Man Upstairs fo' sho!"

"And look at this," continued the woman, "Another miracle! My car is a total wreck, yet this bottle of wine I had in the trunk didn't break. Surely God wants us to drink this wine and celebrate our good fortune."

"Ahm all faw salabrations, me!" said Boudreaux.

She handed the bottle of wine to Boudreaux. He took the bottle, opened it and took several swigs. He passed the bottle back to the woman. She reached for it, immediately put the cap back on and handed it back to Boudreaux.

"Wat's da matta, beb?" inquired Boudreaux. "You ain't goin' take a lil sip, you?"

"Oh no," replied the woman. "I think I'll just sit here and wait for the police!"

Vaguely Familiar

Boudreaux and Chlotilde were driving cross country for their summer vacation. Chlotilde took over the driving to give Boudreaux a rest and was pulled over by the highway patrol.

The officer asked, "Ma'am, did you know you were speeding?"

Chlotilde turned towards Boudreaux and asked, "Wat he say, beb?"

"HE SAY YOU WUZ SPEEDIN', YOU," yelled Boudreaux.

"May I see your license?" asked the patrolman.

Chlotilde again turned to Boudreaux and said, "ennnnnh?"

"HE WANNA SEE YA DRIVA LICENSE, HIM!" shouted Boudreaux.

She took her license out of her purse and handed it to the officer.

"I see you're from Louisiana," said the patrolman. "I spent some time there once and had the worst sex with a woman I've ever had."

"Wat he say?" asked Chlotilde with one hand cupped behind her ear.

"HE SAY HE TINK HE KNO YA !" yelled Boudreaux.

Nobody's Fool

Ole Boudreaux decided his injuries from the accident were serious enough to take the trucking company to court. In court the trucking company's fancy lawyer was questioning Boudreaux.

"Didn't you say at the scene of the accident, 'I'm fine,'?" asked the lawyer.

"Well, ahma tellya wat happened," answered Boudreaux. "Ah had jis loaded my favorite mule, dere, Bessie, inta da......"

"I didn't ask for any details," interrupted the lawyer. "Just answer the question. Did you not say at the scene of the accident, 'I'm fine,'?"

Boudreaux said, "Well, ah had jis got Bessie inta da traila and ah wuz drivin' down da road...."

The lawyer interrupted again and said, "Judge, I am trying to establish the fact that, at the scene of the accident, this man told the state trooper that he was fine. Now several weeks after the accident, he is trying to sue my client. I believe he is a fraud. Please tell him to simply answer the question."

By this time the judge was fairly interested in Boudreaux's answer and told the lawyer, "I'd like to hear what he has to say. Go on, Mr. Boudreaux, tell us your story."

"Tank you, judge," said Boudreaux. "Well, as ah wuz sayin', ah had jis loaded Bessie inta da traila and wuz drivin' down da highway wen dis big, big truck ran da stop sign and smacked my truck rat in da side. Ah wuz tarown inta one ditch and Bessie wuz tarown inta da udda one. Ah wuz hurtin' bad, bad, me, and din wanna move. But ah could hear ole Bessie moaning and groaning, dere, in dat ditch. Ah could tell, me, dat she wuz in tarrible shape jis by da noise she wuz makin'."

"Then what happended?" asked the judge.

"Rat afta da accident happened, a state troopa come dere. We bote could hear Bessie moaning and groaning so, him, he went ova ta hur. Afta he look at hur, he took out his gun and shot hur rat batween da eyes. Den da troopa come across da road wit his gun in his hand and look at me. He said, 'Your mule was in such bad shape I had to shoot her. How are you feeling?'"

All Restrictions Apply

The Judge asked the defendant, "Mr. Boudreaux, do you understand that you have sworn to tell the truth, the whole truth and nothing but the truth?

"May yeah," replied Boudreaux.

"Now what do you say to defend yourself?" questioned the Judge.

"Wit all dem limitations dere, yo hona, not a whole lot!" answered Boudreaux.

Honest Lawyer

An investment counselor decided to leave the company and open her own business. She was shrewd and diligent, so business kept coming in, and soon she realized she needed in-house legal counsel. So she began interviewing various lawyers.

Young Boudreaux had been out of law school for less than one year and was the first to be interviewed.

"As I'm sure you can understand," she said, "In a business like this, our personal integrity must be beyond question." She leaned forward and asked, "Mr. Boudreaux, are you an 'honest' lawyer?"

"Honest? Haaaaaw yeah ahm honest, me!" replied Boudreaux with assurance. "Lemme telya someting abot honesty dere, sha. Ahm so honest, me, dat my papa, him, he lent me fifteen tousand dolla ta git trew lawya skool and, me dere, ah paid him back arry panny da minute ah tried my furst case!"

"That's very impressive, Mr. Boudreaux," said the counselor. "And what sort of case was that?"

"Uuuuuh, my papa, he sued me faw da money," said a squirming Boudreaux.

Shortsighted

Boudreaux and Chlotilde returned home one evening and were shocked to find that their home had been ransacked and burglarized. He quickly telephoned the police and reported the crime.

The police dispatcher broadcast the call to all available units in the area. The department was famous for its K-9 Unit which happened to be close by and was the first on the scene.

As the K-9 officer approached the house with his dog on a leash, Boudreaux ran out on the porch, put his hands on his head and moaned, "Sha lawd, das jis my luck, yeah! Ah call da paleece faw hep and, dem, dey sand me a blind paleeceman!"

Paying With A Smile

Boudreaux was being audited by the IRS and was very unhappy about the situation. He nervously talked with the auditor who came to review the records.

At one point the auditor exclaimed, "Mr. Boudreaux, we feel it's a great privilege to be able to live and work in the United States of America. As a citizen you have the obligation and responsibility to pay taxes, and we expect you to eagerly pay them with a smile."

"Whew, tannnnnk God!" said Boudreaux breathing a sigh of relief. "Ah tought faw a minute dere ya wanted me ta pay wit cash!"

You just might be a Cajun if.....

You have ever used a trash can lid for a pot cover.

You are "gonflayed" after eating a big meal.

Some words you'll probably
never hear a Cajun say.....

"Oh beb, ah got us some tickets faw da opra, dere."

"Ah jis wish, me, dat it would git a lil bit mo' humid in da summa time ova here."

Chapter 7

Boudreaux On Life

Self-Defeating

"Man, you sho look frustrated, you," said Cowan to Boudreaux as they sat drinking beer at the Hubba Hubba.

"You got dat rat, sha," answered Boudreaux

"May wat gotcha so frustrated?" inquired Cowan.

"Ah went ta da booksto dis mornin',dere," explained Boudreaux, "And ah axed da sales lady ware da Self-Help Section wuz. She sed dat if she tolme, it would defeat da purpose!"

Filled With Compassion

Once when Boudreaux was in elementary school, the teacher told the class that she wanted all those who thought they were stupid to stand up. No one stood. She repeated the invitation a second time and again there were no takers. Finally, she told the students that this was going to be their last chance and asked the question a third time.

As she looked around the room, she saw Boudreaux slowly standing up.

With great disappointment she asked, "Boudreaux, do you really believe you're stupid?"

"Sha, lawd, non, teach!" exclaimed Boudreaux. "Ah jis din wanchu standin' up by yosef!"

Rise And Shine

"Oh Boudreaux," said Chlotilde, "Junya don't do nutting but lay in da bed all day long and eat yeast and car wax. Wat's goin' happen ta dat boy?"

"Ah don't kno, me," replied Boudreaux. "Ah guess one day he goin' jis rise and shine!"

Let's Twist Again

Shawee went to visit Boudreaux. As he approached the house, he was puzzled at what he saw through the window. There was a longneck bottle of Budweiser resting on the kitchen table. Boudreaux was standing next to the table going through some crazy gyrations. His body was shaking left and right. His arms were moving wildly in the air and he appeared to be out of control.

Shawee rushed through the door and frantically asked, "May Boudreaux, wat's da matta witchu? You having a fit or someting, you?"

"May non, couyon!" said Boudreaux. "Ahm jis tryin' ta open dis bottle o' beer."

"How you gonna do dat wit dat stoopid stuff ya doin'?" questioned Shawee.

"Ah don't kno, me," said Boudreaux. "But it say rat dere on da bottle, 'twist ta open.'"

No Identify Crisis

A hurricane was threatening the Gulf coast and Boudreaux and his family were forced to go to a designated evacuation shelter. The shelter director was talking to the people in an attempt to make them feel at home. He approached Boudreaux and asked, "Are you an evacuee?"

"Aw non! Ahm a Boudreaux, me," responded Boudreaux.

Misdirected

Chlotilde called Boudreaux on his car phone to convey some information. "You bedda be careful, yeah, beb," cautioned Chlotilde, "Cuz ah jis heard a news flash on da radio, me, dat dey got some nut goin' da wrong way on da I-10!"

"Pooooo, ah can't talk rat na, sha!" responded a frenzied Boudreaux. "But ah kin tellya dis. It ain't jis one, non, it's a whole bunch o' dem!"

Repeat Performance

Boudreaux and Cowan were watching the 10:00 o'clock news. The lead story was about a man sitting on the Mississippi River Bridge threatening to jump. The news camera captured the intense scene as the man pondered his fate.

"Ah betcha a hundred dolla, Boudreaux, dat he gon jump," offered Cowan.

"You gotcha sef a bet, sha," countered Boudreaux.

As they continued to watch, the would-be jumper decided to take the plunge into the river causing Boudreaux to lose the bet. He handed a one hundred dollar bill to Cowan.

"Boudreaux, ah can't take ya money, me," said a guilt-ridden Cowan. "Ta tellya da troot ah wuz watchin' da 6:00 o'clock news and dey showed him jumping den."

"May me, too, ah wuz watching!" said Boudreaux. "But ah nava tought he wuz goin' be stoopid enuff ta jump agin, him!"

Prime Example

Walking down Camp Street in New Orleans, Boudreaux was approached by a derelect who asked him for two dollars.

"Ah betcha goin' go buy yosef some booze, you, if ah give ya dat money, huh?" asked Boudreaux.

"No," replied the bum.

"Den ya probly goin' gamble it away on dem video poka machine, you," said Boudreaux.

"No," was the reply again.

Putting his hand on the derelect's shoulder, Boudreaux said, "Look, if ah give ya da two dolla, dere, you tink ya could come hume wit me so Chlotilde kin see wat happen ta a man who don't drink or gamble!"

Quick Thinker

Boudreaux and Chlotilde were sitting on the front porch swing after supper. Suddenly a stranger jumped in Boudreaux's truck and began speeding away. Boudreaux was furious and jumped from the swing in hot pursuit. Ten minutes later he returned and had a big smile on his face.

"You caught'm, huh beb?" said Chlotilde.

"Aw non," replied Boudreaux.

"Den how come ya got dat big smile on ya face, you?" asked Chlotilde.

"Cuz ah got da numba on da license plate!" said Boudreaux proudly.

Making It Worthwhile

Boudreaux and Cowan were at the dance, a fais-do-do, one Saturday night. As usual, they consumed at least one beer per dance. Nature soon called and they both went to the restroom to relieve themselves. As they walked up to the urinals, Boudreaux pulled his hand out of his pocket. A quarter came out, too, and fell in the urinal. Boudreaux quickly pulled out his wallet, took out a twenty dollar bill and dropped it in with the quarter.

"Couyon! How come you done someting so stoopid like dat?" asked a puzzled Cowan.

"Maaaaay, you don't tink dat ahm goin' put my hand in dat messy ting dere faw jis a quarta?" replied Boudreaux.

Anything You Can Do I Can Do Better

Boudreaux once had a job as a taxicab driver in Baton Rouge. One day he picked up a Texien on his way to the airport. When they passed by the LSU football stadium the Texien asked, "What's that, partner?"

"May dat's Tiger Stadium," answered Boudreaux. "Dey call it Deat Valley cuz a lota teems usta git killed in dere."

"How long did it take yall to build it?" drawled the Texien.

"Uuuuuuh, bot five years, ah guess," responded Boudreaux.

"We've got a bigger one in Austin that only took one year," bragged the Texien.

As they passed the state capitol, the Texien again inquired,

"What's that building?"

"Dat's da state captol," answered Boudreaux. "Dey probly got mo crooks in dere den dey got in Angola."

"And how long did it take yall to build that?" asked the Texien.

"Bot teree years," retorted Boudreaux.

"We've got one in Austin that only took six months," said the Texien with a smirk.

At this point Boudreaux just about had enough. As they drove past the Mississippi River Bridge, the Texien once again asked, "How long did it take yall to build that bridge?"

"Ah don't kno faw sho, but ah kin tellya dis. It wudn't dere dis mornin' wen ah passed!" replied Boudreaux.

Smelly Situation

Boudreaux and Chlotilde were going to visit some relatives in north Louisiana. Chlotilde was driving in order to give Boudreaux a much needed break. As they were enjoying the scenery, a skunk ran right in front of the car, and she was unable to avoid hitting it. Feeling somewhat guilty, she pulled over on the side of the road to check it out. The skunk was squirming around and obviously in much pain. Chlotilde, upset that the animal was hurt, picked him up and tried desperately to calm him down and give comfort.

"May Boudreaux," said Chlotilde with tears in her eyes, "Wat kin ah do ta stop'm from squirmin' around like dat and ta take away some o' da peen?"

"Jis put'm unda yo arm and hold'm dere faw a lil while," answered Boudreaux. "Dat oughta do it."

"But beb, wat abot da smell?" asked Chlotilde.

"Jis hold his nose, Chlotilde, and da smell shouldn't bodda him dat much!" replied Boudreaux.

Historical Mistake

Junya was walking along the bayou behind his house early one morning. Suddenly he noticed that the family outhouse, located on the bank, was tilting dangerously towards the bayou.

The heavy downpour from the previous night had seriously eroded the bank where the outhouse was located. Reasoning that the outhouse was beyond salvage, Junya began whacking it with a big stick and then pushed it into the bayou. He watched as it quickly sank into the muddy water.

A few hours later, Boudreaux rushed towards Junya and asked angrily, "Oh JUNYA! You da one dat push da outhouse in da bayou, dere?"

"Papa," answered the boy, "Jis like George Washington, ah can't tell a lie. It wuz me dat done it."

"Din come wit me ta da back o' da house," said Boudreaux, "Cuz you goin' git da whippin' o' yo life, boy!"

Junya was shocked by the turn of events and pleaded, "But papa, wen George Washington tol his papa dat he wuz da one dat chop down dat charry tree, dere, his papa din give him no whippin'."

"Aw non, but his papa wudn't in dat charry tree wen he chop it down, edda!" explained Boudreaux.

No Free Ride

Boudreaux and Chlotilde went to California on vacation. While there, they decided they wanted to see the homes of their favorite movie stars. He called a cab instead of renting a car.

When the cab arrived, the driver asked, "Do you want to take the scenic route or are you in a hurry?"

"Maaaaay, ah guess we kinna in a hurry, us," replied Boudreaux.

"Then you'll want to go the freeway," answered the cabbie.

"May non, we goin' pay cash, us!" said Boudreaux.

Way Off Base

Boudreaux and Chlotilde were walking through the mall. They came upon one of those penny scales that tell you your fortune as well as your weight. Boudreaux stepped on the scale and dropped his coin in the slot. Out popped a small white card.

"Lissen ta dis, beb," said Boudreaux as he viewed the card. "It say dat ah got planny anergy, ahm smart, smart, me, and ahma great luva!"

"Aw yeah, and it probly gotcha weight wrong, too, huh!" answered Chlotilde with a smirk.

You're In Good Hands

Boudreaux and Chlotilde were in Hawaii on vacation. He was sitting by the pool, soaking in some rays and sipping a beer. Not one to stay quiet very long, he began a conversation with the guy sitting next to him.

"May how ya doin', dere, Cap?" asked Boudreaux. "My neem is Boudreaux. Ahm from da bayou and ahm here on vacation, me. My house caught on fiyuh, dere, and burn ta da ground. Ah got me a lil extra money from da insurance money so ah taut ahd take da wife ova here ta pass a good time."

"Well that's interesting," responded the guy. "I'm here from California. My house flooded and I used the extra insurance money for this vacation."

"Dat sho is intresting, yeah," replied Boudreaux. "But lemme axe you dis. How in da heck you start a flood?"

Winning The Dough

Boudreaux went into a restaurant, ordered a cup of coffee and sat down to drink it. He looked on the side of the cup and found a peel-off prize.

He pulled off the tab and yelled, "Ah won! Ah really won! Ah won a mota home, me!"

The waitress hurried over and said, "That's impossible, Boudreaux. The biggest prize given away in this contest is a mini van!"

"Haw non!" shouted Boudreaux. "Ah won me a mota home!"

By this time the manager had made his way to the table and said, "You couldn't possibly have won a motor home because we didn't have that as a prize!"

"Dere ain't no mistake, sha!" exclaimed Boudreaux. "Ah won me a mota home, and it's rat dere on da ticket as pleen as da day!"

The manager took the winning ticket from Boudreaux and examined it. It read, "WIN A BAGEL."

Memory Challenged

Boudreaux and Chlotilde had been married for a very long time and had reached the age of eighty. They were both having problems remembering things, so they decided to go to Dr. Fontenot for a checkup to make sure nothing was wrong with them.

When they arrived at Dr. Fontenot's office, they explained to him about the problem they were having with their memory. After a thorough examination, he said, "You're both okay physically, but you might want to start writing things down and making notes to help you remember things." They thanked Dr. Fontenot and went home.

Later that night while watching TV, Boudreaux got up from his chair and Chlotilde asked, "May ware you goin'?"

"Ta da kitchen," replied Boudreaux.

"Kinya bring me a bowl o' iscream?" asked Chlotilde.

"May yeah!" responded Boudreaux.

"You don't tink dat maybe you oughta rat it down so ya kin remamba?" questioned Chlotilde.

"Haaaaaw non!" answered Boudreaux. "It's jis a lil bowl o' iscream you want. Ah kin remamba dat, me."

"Den how bot you put some strawbarry on da top," requested Chlotilde.

"Das no prablum, beb," said Boudreaux.

"Din faw sho ya batta rat dat down, yeah, cuz ah kno' you goin' fogit, you," cautioned Chlotilde.

"Ah kin remamba dat," replied Boudreaux. "Ahm not no idiot, non, me! You wanna a bowl o' iscream wit strawbarry on da top."

"Tellya wat," continued Chlotilde. "How bot you put a lil shot o' whip cream on top o' da strawbarry dere. But Boudreaux, ah kno how you are yeah, you. You batta rat it down, yeah!"

"Oh beb," said Boudreaux with irritation in his voice. "Ah don't needa rat it down, non. Ah kin remamba doze few tings you want, yeah, me."

Some twenty minutes later Boudreaux returned from the kitchen and handed her a plate of bacon and eggs.

Chlotilde stared at the plate for a moment then said in disgust, "You fogot my toast, you!"

Special Standards

Boudreaux was a young man and thought it was time for him to find a wife and settle down. He thought the quickest way to accomplish this might be to put an ad in the local newspaper. It read: "Aligible batchla lookin' faw a woman who kin cook, sew, take care o' da house and who got a boat and outboard mota. Pleez sand foto of boat and mota!"

A Cold Lesson

Boudreaux and Chlotilde moved north, to Minnesota, when his company transferred him. He wrote short notes daily on postcards to his "podna," Shawee, to keep him informed of what was happening.

Dec. 16 - "Shawee, it started ta sno a lot up here. Dis is da furst sno me and Chlotilde done seen in a long, long time, us. We took out some hot buttered rum and sat by da pitcha winda watchin' da sno flakes come down on da trees and coverin' da ground. Cot dawg, dat's some purty, yeah!"

Dec. 17 - "Shawee, we woke up dis mornin', us, wit sno on da ground. Ah shoveled sno from da driveway faw da furst time and ah like it a lot, me. Da snoplow machine come by and accidently covered my driveway wit sno. Da driva, he smiled, him, and waved. Ah smiled back, me, and shoveled da sno agin."

Dec. 18 - "Shawee, it snowed five mo' inches las nite and da tampachure drop down ta nine degrees. Dis is goose and duck whetta — ah goose Chlotilde and duck unda da cova agin. Man, it's some cold in dis place, yeah. A few limbs on da trees broke off and fell in da yard. Da snoplow, he come by and did his lil trick agin — shoveled da brownish-gray sno on my driveway."

Dec. 19 - Da tampachure went up jis enuff ta melt da sno den it drop eight degrees and made some ice. Ah went ta buy some sno tires faw da caw and fell on my butt. Hadta pay da dockta $145.00. Some mo' sno is axpected."

Dec. 20 - Cooooot dawg, Shawee, iiiiit's COLD!!! Ahm freezin' my butt off, me! Sold da caw and bought a 4 x 4 ta git ta work. Slid inta da guardrail and did $2200 wert o' damage. Had anudda eight inches o' dat damn sno las nite. Dat stoopid snoplow come by two times taday. Na da driveway ain't nuttin' but ice. Ahm gittin' planny fed up wit dis whetta, me!"

Dec. 21 - "Shawee, pooooo, some mo' sno and it's saven degrees below ZERO! Sha lawd, all da trees los dere limbs las nite and teree trees wuz broke in half. Da lectricity went off, too. Tried ta keep from freezin' my butt off by huggin' Choltilde's, but hur's wuz jis as cold as mine. Ah tried ta keep warm by using some candles. Hadta git up in da middle o' da nite ta go ta da battrum wit no heat. It sho' remind me o' da good ole days back home, yeah! My butt got stuck ta da toilet seat. Ah got scared, me, and got up fast, fast. Ah knock dem candles offa da stand and caught da curtins on fiyuh. Ah put out da fiyuh but got sacand degree burns on my hands. While comin' back from da dockta, my 4 x 4 slid on da ice and wuz totaled. Damn, ah hate dis whetta, yeah!"

Dec. 22 - "Shawee, dat dam sno jis keep comin' down! Hadta put on all da clothes ah own jis ta git ta da doggone mailbox. If ah aver ketch dat SOB dat drive dat snoplow, ahm goin' wring his neck, yeah! Da powa still off, toilet frozen, and part o' da roof done caved in. Some mo' sno predicted!"

Dec. 23 - "Shawee, six mo' inches o' damn sno came down wit sleet. Who knows wat udda kinda stuff goin' fall taday. Ah went outside, me, ta clear da driveway and da snoplow driva come by and dump mo' sno on my driveway. Ah chase'm and stop'm jis long enuff ta whip his behind. Ah wuz gonna hit'm wit my shovel, but he got away. Ah guess he could see in my eyes dat ah ment bidness, cuz he run like hell, him. Chlotilde done lef me. Da rent caw don't wanna start. Me, ahm goin' sno blind and my toes dey frozen! Mo' sno predicted and da wind chill is fawty-fo' degrees below zero. Cot dawg it's cold!"

Dec. 24 - "Shawee, ahma see ya faw Christmas, bro, cuz ahm movin' back ta da bayou, me! Ah jis can't take dis no mo!"

Out Smarted

Boudreaux, Shawee, Kymon and Cowan were enrolled in an organic chemistry class at Tulane University. They did so well on all the quizzes, midterms and labs, that they each had an "A" for the semester. They were so confident that they decided to go up to LSU and party with some friends the weekend before finals.

After all the hardy-partying, they slept all day Sunday and didn't make it back to New Orleans until Monday morning. Since they were late for the final, they decided to make an excuse to the professor so they could take a make-up exam. Later in the day, they found their professor and explained that they had gone to LSU for the weekend, but unfortunately, had a flat tire on the way back. They also told him that they didn't have a spare and couldn't get help for a long time. As a result, they missed the final.

The professor thought it over and then agreed they could make up the final the following day. The four Cajun boys were elated and relieved. They studied hard that night and went in the next day at the time the professor had told them. He placed them in separate rooms, handed each of them a test booklet and told them to begin.

They looked at the first problem. It was worth five points and was something simple about free radical formation. "Coooot dawg! We're in luck us!" they thought at the same time, each one in his separate room. "Dis goin' be as easy as eatin' a piece o' boudin!"

Each finished the problem and then turned the page. On the second page was written: For ninety-five points: Which tire?

Local Scholar

Two tourists were driving through north Louisiana. As they were approaching Natchitoches, they started arguing about the pronunciation of the town. They argued back and forth until they stopped for lunch.

As they stood at the counter, Boudreaux was in line next to them. One of the tourists turned to him and said, "Sir, before we order, could you please settle an argument for us? Would you please pronounce where we are.....very, very slowly?"

"Haw yeah," replied Boudreaux. "It's Burrrrgerrrrrr Kiiiinnng!"

Wasted Gift

Chlotilde's birthday was rapidly approaching, and Boudreaux was trying to decide on a gift. He wasn't sure what to get her so he chose something unusual. He went to Falgout Funeral Home and purchased a complete funeral package for her. He picked out the casket, the flowers, the mausoleum slot, the songs and even made arrangements with the parish priest. He presented her with a birthday card which explained the nature of the gift.

"Oh beb, ah don't kno wat ta say, me," said Chlotilde in shock. "Ah ain't nava got nuttin' like dis befo'."

"You ain't gotta say a ting, sha," said Boudreaux proudly. "Ah jis wanted ta do someting different faw you ta make dis da mos spacial birtday dat you nava did have."

Needless to say Chlotilde was speechless. Life, however, went on as usual and Chlotilde's birthday was at hand again. The birthday came and went with no present from Boudreaux. Chlotilde was quite hurt and it was more than she could stand. She confronted him about his lack of consideration.

"How come you din buy me no birtday present, you?" asked Chlotilde

"Maaaaay, why should ah?" asked Boudreaux. "You din even use da one ah gave ya las year!"

Die Hard

An angry Boudreaux went back to the garage where he'd purchased an expensive battery for his car six months earlier.

"Look here, Cap!" said a disgruntled Boudreaux. "Wen ah bought dis battry you tolme dat it would be da las one my caw would aver need. Na it done died on me afta only six munts, dere!"

"I'm sorry," said the garage owner apologetically, "But I didn't think your car would last longer than that."

Chip Off The Ole Block

Boudreaux's son, Junya, was a real handful as a youngster. Once, when he was eight years old, he swaggered into a lounge and demanded of the barmaid, "Gimme a double shot o' Scotch on da rocks, dere, sha!"

"What do you want to do, get me in trouble?" the barmaid asked.

"Maybe lata, beb," said Junya. "But rat na jis gimme da Scotch."

Life Goes On

An elderly Chlotilde met a friend of hers, Suzette, at the supermarket whom she had not seen in a long time. They inquired about each other's health, and then Suzette asked Chlotilde how Boudreaux was doing.

"Oh may Boudreaux, him, he died jis las week," explained Chlotilde. "He wuz in da garden diggin' up a cabbage faw dinna, hada big heart attack and drop down dead rat dere in da middle o' da vegetibble patch!"

"Ahm so varry sorry, me," said Suzette. "Wat didja do?"

"Jis opened up me a can o' peas instead," answered Chlotilde calmly.

Good Samaritan

Seeing a car rolling down the street with no one in the driver's seat, Boudreaux ran to the car, opened the door, jumped in and applied the brakes.

"Cooooot dawg, ah finely got dis ting stop!" Boudreaux proclaimed proudly to Gaston who appeared on the scene.

"May ah kno," said a breathless Gaston. "Ah wuz pushin' it, me!"

Imagine That

Boudreaux signed the receipt for his credit card purchase, but the clerk noticed that he had never signed his name on the back of the card.

"I'm sorry, Mr. Boudreaux, but I can't complete this transaction unless the card is signed," said the clerk.

"May how come?" asked Boudreaux.

"Because it's necessary to compare the signature on the credit card with the one on the receipt," explained the clerk.

"May jis give it here, beb, ahma sign it, me," said Boudreaux taking the card.

She carefully compared this signature with the one on the receipt.

"Dey match?" asked Boudreaux.

A Little Confused

The bank robbers arrived just before closing and promptly ordered the few remaining customers, the tellers, clerks, and guards to disrobe and lie face down on the floor behind the counter. Boudreaux and Chlotilde had the misfortune of being there, and it was a frightening experience to say the least. Chlotilde was so nervous that she pulled off all her clothes and lay down on the floor facing up.

"Cot dawg, beb, turn ova," whispered Boudreaux. "Dis here is a stick-up, not da office party, non!"

Paradise Lost

As a young man went to lunch, he noticed an elderly man, Boudreaux, some seventy-five to eighty years old sitting on a bench near the shopping center. He was crying uncontrollably. The man stopped and asked Boudreaux what was wrong.

"Ah got me a twanny-two year old wife at hume," said Boudreaux. "She make luv ta me arry mornin', and den she git up, hur, and make me some lost bread, sausage, fresh fruit and freshly ground brewed coffee."

"Then why are you crying?" asked the young man.

"And den she make me some humemade soup faw lunch and my mos bestess brownies. And den she make luv ta me hafa da aftanoon," replied Boudreaux.

"Well, why are you crying?" asked the young man again.

"Faw suppa, dere, she make me a furst class meal wit my Budweiser and some bread puddin'," responded Boudreaux. "And den she make luv ta me til 2:00 o'clock in da mornin'."

"For God sake, why in the world would you be crying?" asked the young man in disbelief.

"CUZ AH CAN'T REMAMBA WARE AH LIVE, ME!!!" explained Boudreaux.

Family Matters

Gaston noticed that Boudreaux was looking a little depressed and wanted to see if he could help.

"Oh Boudreaux," said Gaston, "Ya look a lil down, you. Wat's da prablum, sha?"

"Well, ta telya da troot," said Boudreaux, "Ahm gon be a fadda."

"May das some good news!" replied Gaston. "Ya oughta be axcited, you. Ah betcha Chlotilde is?"

"May non! She don't kno nuttin' abot it yet!" explained Boudreaux.

Like A Good Neighbor

Boudreaux and Chlotilde were asleep when they heard a loud banging on the front door. He rolled over, looked at the clock and saw that it was half-past three in the morning.

"Ahm sho not gon git outa my bed at dis time o' nite," thought Boudreaux as he turned over.

Suddenly, there was an even louder banging on the door.

"Ya not gon ansa dat, you?" asked Chlotilde.

Without saying a word, Boudreaux dragged himself out of bed and went to the door. Opening it, he found a man standing on the porch. It didn't take Boudreaux long to realize that the man was drunk.

"H-h-h-h-hi, there," slurred the stranger. "K-k-k-kinya gimme a push?"

"Ah - guess - not!" shouted Boudreaux. "It's haf-pas teree in da mornin' and ah wuz in bed, me! Git da heck outa here!"

Boudreaux slammed the door, went back to bed and told Chlotilde what happened.

She said, "Ya kno, dat wudn't too nice, non, beb. Remamba da nite, dere, we wuz comin' from da show in da pouring down reen and da caw stop on us? And ya hadta knock on dat man's door ta git some hep ta start da caw? Wat wooda happen ta us, dere, if heda tol us ta git loss?"

"Ah remamba dat, me, but dis guy here wuz drunk!" argued Boudreaux.

"Dat don't make no matta," countered Chlotilde. "Dat man needed our hep, him, and it would be da Christian ting ta do." Boudreaux reluctantly got out of bed again, got dressed and walked to the door. He opened the door but didn't see the stranger. He shouted, "Hey Cap, you still want dat push, you?" He heard a voice cry out, "Aw yeah, p-p-p-pleez!" "May ware you at, you?" asked an irritated Boudreaux. "R-r-r-r-rat ova here on yo s-s-s-swing!" answered the stranger.

Complete Job

Gaston stopped by Boudreaux's house and found him feverishly working on the lock on the driver's side of the car.

"Watcha doin', dere?" asked Gaston.

"Aw, Chlotilde, hur, she done locked da doggone keys in da caw," replied Boudreaux.

As Gaston watched from the passenger side, he instinctively tried the door handle and discovered it was open.

"Hey, Boudreaux, looka dis. It's open!" announced Gaston.

"May ah kno dat, me," answered Boudreaux. "Ah done alreddy got dat side!"

Double Trouble

Boudreaux and Chlotilde were back from their honeymoon only two weeks when he came home from work with a surprise announcement.

"Oh beb, ah invited fo' o' da fellas from work ta suppa on Friday nite, me," said Boudreaux.

"How couldja do dat ta me?" asked Chlotilde frantically. "Ya kno ah ain't dat good a cook, me!"

"Well, ta tellya da troot, sha, dere gon be eight people," confessed Boudreaux, "Cuz each one o' dem's gon bring his ole lady."

"Wat ahma do, Boudreaux?" asked a tearful Chlotilde. "Talk abot a mess ya done got me in dis time, you!"

"Look, it ain't gon be dat bad non, beb," assured Boudreaux. "Ahma git my mama ta cook a big pot o' gumbo and maka potata salid. Ahma pick up us a coupla loafs o' Franch bred at da bakry. Den all ya gotta do, dere, is bake a lil cake faw desert."

That sounded reasonable to Chlotilde, and she was able to regain her composure.

Friday morning Chlotilde called Boudreaux at work in tears. "Dis ain't gon work, non, beb!" she cried hysterically. "Da only cake racipe ah got, me, feed only six!"

"May cot dawg, Chlotilde, den jis double da racipe!" said Boudreaux. "Dis ain't no rocket science we talkin' abot here, non!"

At four o'clock Boudreaux got another phone call from his better half. She was frantic. "Ah jis can't do dis, me!" cried Chlotilde. "Ahm tellin' ya it ain't gon work!"

"Naaaaa wat's da matta?" asked Boudreaux in frustration.

"Da racipe say ta use two eggs, dere," replied Chlotilde.

"Maaaaay, den use fo' egg!" explained Boudreaux. "Ya gott'm, huh?"

"Yeah, ah gott'm, but it say ta use fo' cup o' flour," responded Chlotilde.

"Den use eight cup o' flour faw God sake!" answered Boudreaux testily. "Wat's da prablum?"

"Da prablum ain't da ingredients, sha," cried Chlotilde. "It's jis dat da cake gotta be baked at 350 degrees and ah checked da oven two times, me. Dere ain't kno way faw me ta turn up da heat ta 700 degrees!"

No Sympathy

Boudreaux finally won the Louisiana Lottery after playing it for many years. The jackpot was five million dollars.

Several months went by, and the staff at the local United Way office realized that it had not received a donation from him.

The person in charge of contributions called Boudreaux to persuade him to contribute. She said, "Mr. Boudreaux, our records show that out of a five million dollar jackpot, you haven't given a penny to charity. Wouldn't you like to give back to the community in some way?"

Boudreaux mulled over this for a moment and replied, "Furst

o' all, sha, didja records show ya dat my mama's dying afta a real long sickness and hur medical bills, dere, dey sky high?"

Embarassed, the United Way representative mumbled, "Uuuuuh, no."

"Or faw dat matta," continued Boudreaux, "Dat my brudda, who's a disabled vetrun, he's blind, him, and gotta stay in a wheelchair?"

The United Way representative began to stammer out an apology, but was interrupted when Boudreaux asked, "Or dat my sista's husbun died in a caw wreck leavin' hur wit nuttin' and teree lil chiren?"

The red-face representative, completely beaten, said simply, "I had no idea..."

On a roll, Boudreaux cut her off again and said, "So if ah don't give no money ta dem, how come ya tink ahm gon give some ta you?"

Sophisticated Recipes

While Boudreaux was still a bachelor, he and Gaston were talking one morning over a cup of coffee. It didn't take long for the conversation to drift from politics to cooking.

"Ah bought me a cookbook once, yeah," said Boudreaux. "But ah could nava do nuttin' wit it, me."

"Too much fancy work in it, eh?" asked Gaston.

"Haw yeah," said Boudreaux. "Arry one o' dem doggone recipes dere started off da seem way — take a clean dish!"

Working Flashers

Boudreaux's car broke down on I-10 one day, so he pulled off on the shoulder. He stepped out of the car and opened the trunk. Out jumped two men in trench coats. They walked to the rear of the vehicle and stood facing oncoming traffic. They began opening their coats and exposing themselves to approaching drivers.

Not surprisingly, one of the worst pile-ups in the history of I-10 occurred. It's wasn't long before a trooper showed up. The trooper, clearly enraged, ran toward Boudreaux and yelled, "What in the heck is going on here?"

"May, my caw broke down," explained Boudreaux.

"Well, what in the world are these two perverts doing here by the road?" yelled the trooper.

"Dem? Dey jis my emergency flashas!" replied Boudreaux.

The Name Game

Chlotilde went to the doctor's office for a checkup. She filled out the patient-information form required by the office. After reviewing the form, the nurse asked, "Mrs. Boudreaux, how many children do you have?"

"Ah got tan chiren, me, jis like ah put on dat paper, dere," answered Chlotilde.

"And what are their names?" asked the nurse.

"Junya, Junya, Junya, Junya, Junya, Junya, Junya, Junya, Junya and Junya," replied Chlotilde.

"They're all named Junya?" inquired the nurse.

"Haw yeah," responded Chlotilde.

"What if you want them to come in from playing outside?" questioned the nurse.

"May das easy, sha," said Chlotilde. "Ah jis call 'Junya' and dey all come runnin' inside."

"And if you want them to come to the table for supper?" queried the nurse.

"Ah jis say, Junya, come eat yo suppa," explained Chlotilde.

"But what if you just want ONE of them to do something?" she asked.

"Maaaaay, das easy, too," replied Chlotilde. "Ah jis use dere las neem!"

The Naked Truth

As the police were making their rounds downtown one night, they noticed someone loitering around the courthouse. As they came closer, they could see that it was a man, and he didn't have on any clothes. Approaching him, they realized it was Boudreaux.

"Good God, Boudreaux!" exclaimed one of the officers. "What in the world are you doing here without any clothes?"

"Well Cap," answered Boudreaux, "Ah wuz at dis pawty, dere, and da host tol arrybody ta take off dair clothes an git neckked. Den he put out da lite and say faw arrybody ta go ta town. Ah mus be fas, me, cuz ahm da furst one ta git here."

You just might be a Cajun if.....

You have more than one relative whose first name is "T" or "Boo".

You have relatives whose first names are "Taunt" and "Nonk".

Some words you'll probably never hear a Cajun say.....

"Cot dawg, dat wedding reception lasted too long, yeah!"

"Pooooo, dis sauce piquant is way too peppery faw me ta eat!"

Chapter 8

Boudreaux On Philosophy

Venus And Mars

Boudreaux and Kymon were engaged in conversation over a cup of community coffee.

"Cot dawg," said Boudreaux, "Men and wamans, dere, dey so different, dem."

"May watcha mean?" asked Kymon.

"Take sax faw instance," said Boudreaux.

"Ah sho do! Anytime, anywares, me!" blurted Kymon.

"Dere ya go!   Dat's jis wat ah meen," said Boudreaux. "Wamans, dey needa reason ta have sax, dem. Us, we jis needa place!"

On Second Thought

Boudreaux's backyard shed burned to the ground and his wife, Chlotilde, called the insurance company to make a claim.

"We had dat shed insured, us, faw fifty tousand dolla," said Chlotilde to the agent, "And ah want my money, me!"

"Hold on there, Chlotilde," said the agent. "Insurance doesn't work quite like that. We'll need to conduct an investigation, determine the value of what was insured, and then provide you with a new one of comparable worth."

There was a long pause, then Chlotilde replied, "Den ahd like ta cancel da policy on my husbun, Boudreaux!"

Food For Thought

Boudreaux and Cowan were walking home late one night from the Hubba Hubba. Naturally, they were feeling no pain and in a reflective mood.

Looking up at the sky, Cowan pondered, "Ah wunda, me, if dey got intelligent life on some o'dem udda planets?"

"Huh, me dere, sometime ah wunda if dey got intelligent life on dis one!" responded Boudreaux.

Magic Cards

Boudreaux and T-Brud were drinking a few cold ones at the Hubba Hubba. As usual, they were engaged in intellectual conversation.

"Ah wunda, me, if people kin really predict da fucha wit cards?" asked T-Brud.

"Haw yeah, Chlotilde kin, hur," replied Boudreaux.

"Geeeeet ouuuuut!" said a skeptical T-Brud.

"Huh, ah seen hur do it planny times, me," said Boudreaux. "She kin take one look, dere, at Junya's report card and kin tell'm zackly wat's goin' happen ta him wen ah git hume."

Age-Old Question

Boudreaux and Cowan were involved in a discussion over a cup of Community coffee.

"Lemme axe you dis," said Boudreaux. "If a man is in da woods all by hissef and dere ain't no woman aroun' nowares ta hear him, and if he say someting out loud, den would he still be wrong?"

Something To Talk About

"Oh Kymon," said Boudreaux taking a swig from his Bud, "Doya aver stop ta tink abot some o' da stoopid tings dat people say, dem?"

"All da time," answered Kymon. "It's arryware — on da talavision, da radio, dem bumpa sticka and even here at da Hubba Hubba. How dey come up wit dem dum tings, me, ah don't kno."

"Huh, ah don't kno me edda," responded Boudreaux. "But dey sho do."

"Haw yeah," said Kymon. "Like 'save da whales, collect da whole set' and 'on da udda hand, you got different fingas.'"

"Ah kno watcha meen, sha," said Boudreaux. "Some ah seen, me, is 'ah got lost in tought, it wuz unfamiliar territory', 'honk if ya luv peace and quiet' and ' 'scuse my drivin', ahm reloading.' Das crazy, huh?"

"Faw sho," replied Kymon, "But dat don't stop'em, non. Dey jis keep on comin'. Like 'despite da coss o' livin', it's still planny popular' and 'he who laughs las, tinks da slowest.'"

"You'd tink dat dey would try ta do someting mo' constructive wit dere life," remarked Boudreaux.

"Kinna like us, huh," replied Kymon.

"Yeah ya rat!" said Boudreaux. "Hey Cap, bring us a coupla mo' Buds ova here, huh!"

A Practical Outlook

Boudreaux took Chlotilde to the airshow at the Belle Chase Naval Station. Watching with much excitement, she told Boudreaux she wanted to ride in one of the planes.

"But, beb, dat coss tan dolla! Das a lota money, yeah!" exclaimed Boudreaux.

"Yabbut, if you really luv me you goin' git me dat ride," responded Chlotilde.

"Look, tan dolla is tan dolla!" retorted Boudreaux.

She kept bugging Boudreaux about the ride until one of the pilots overheard the conversation. He figured he could have a little fun with them.

He went up to Boudreaux and Chlotilde and said, "I tell you what I'll do. If you and your husband can ride the whole airplane ride without saying a word, I'll give YOU ten dollars!"

"Dat sho sound lika good deal ta me, cuz tan dolla is tan dolla!" said Boudreaux excitedly. "Go hed and git in da pleen, beb!"

The pilot took off with both of them on board. He began doing all kinds of dives, turns and rollarounds in the air. He flew upside down, sideways, and even made the plane do a big loop right at the end. He didn't hear anything from either Boudreaux or Chlotilde so he landed the plane.

Boudreaux hopped out of the plane and the pilot told him, "I thought sure you were going to say something!"

"Well, Cap, ta tellya da troot dere, " responded Boudreaux, "Ah almos sed someting, me, when Chlotilde fell outa da pleen da las time you turn it upside down. Butchu kno wat dey say, sha, tan dolla is tan dolla!"

Good, Better, Best

T-Brud stopped by Boudreaux's house for a cup of coffee and a little conversation.

"Oh T-Brud," said Boudreaux, "Ah jis made me a fresh batch o' boudin, dere. You want some, you?"

"It's good?" asked T-Brud.

"Good? Shaaaaa, my boudin, dere, is jis like sax. Some is mo betta den uddas, but dere ain't no such ting as a bad one, non!" bragged Boudreaux with a big smile.

Pondering Thoughts

Boudreaux, Kymon and Cowan were at the Hubba Hubba engaged in their favorite pastime. After a few hours and many brews, they began to get philosophical.

"Cot dawg, dere's some tings ah don't undastan, non, me," said Boudreaux as he paid for another round of beer.

"May like wat?" asked Kymon.

"Maaaaay, a coupla tings, dere," answered Boudreaux. "Like... befo' dey invanted da drawing board, wat dey went back to? And... if da #2 pancil is da mos popla, how come it's still numba two?"

"Sha lawd, you got too much time on ya hands, you," commented Kymon. "You needa spand mo' time drinkin' beer instead o' havin' dem stoopid toughts."

"Aw yeah, you call dem stoopid, you, cuz ya can't ansa dem," laughed Boudreaux. "But me, dere, ah tink a lot, yeah. Like... if work is so great, how come dey gotta pay ya ta do it? And... if all da world's a stage, ware's da audience sittin', dem? And den...

why dey call it tourist season if we can't shoot at'em? Ansa dat, couyon, and ahm goin' buy da next roun' agin."

"If you jis keep yo mout shut, you, ahm goin't buy da beers faw da rast o' da nite!" responded Cowan.

"You got yosef a deal, dere, Cap," said a jubilant Boudreaux. "But jis remamba dis, don't sweat da petty tings and don't pet da sweaty tings!"

Far Enough

A hurricane was in the Gulf and headed straight for bayou country. Boudreaux knew the threat was real, and it was time to flee to safety. So he summoned the family together, packed some clothing and other items and strapped a pirogue to the top of his car. He drove to I-55 and headed north away from the dreaded hurricane as fast as possible.

After traveling for a few hours, he stopped at a gas station in a small town to tank up. The attendant asked, "Ware you goin' wit dat pirogue on top o' ya caw, you?"

"We gittin' away from da hurrikeen, us," answered Boudreaux, "And we got sumo ta go."

When the gas gauge registered empty, he once again stopped to tank up. The station hand inquired, "Why you got dat pirogue, dere, tied ta da top o' ya caw?"

"We vacuatin' from dat hurrikeen, and we ain't gone far enuff yet," replied Boudreaux.

After several additional hours of hard driving, more gas was needed. Boudreaux stopped at a service station. As the employee was pumping the gas, he asked, "How come ya got dat doggone pirogue on top o' yo caw like dat?"

"We on da run, us, and jis tryin' ta stay ahed o' dat hurrikeen," responded Boudreaux.

Boudreaux "put the petal to the metal" and was making great time. But the inevitable happened; the gas tank was almost empty. He turned off on the next exit and was fortunate enough to find a gas station close by. The attendant asked with a puzzled look on his face, "What the heck you got up on top of your car partner?"

"Well, Chlotilde, ah tink we done gone far enuff, us," said Boudreaux with a sigh of relief. "We goin' be safe here, beb!"

The Other Side

Boudreaux and T-Brud were sitting on the banks of the bayou but on opposite sides.

"Hey, Boudreaux!" shouted T-Brud. "How are tings on da udda side o' da bayou, dere?"

"May you oughta kno," responded Boudreaux. "You on da udda side, you!"

Life Sentence

Shawee and Boudreaux were helping to promote business at the Hubba Hubba by spending a large portion of their paycheck there. As usual, the conversation became philosophical as the beer became plentiful.

"You kno, Boudreaux, ah heard on da news las nite dat da shortest santence in da Anglish language is 'ah am'," commented Shawee.

"Huh, ah don't kno bot dat, me," countered Boudreaux. "But ah kin sho tellya wat da longest santence is."

"Wat?" asked Shawee.

"Ah do!" lamented Boudreaux.

The Cajun Twelve Days of Christmas

As Boudreaux expressed his love for Chlotilde during the Christmas season, she responded to each of his offerings on a daily basis.

Day 1

Dear Boudreaux, Tank you faw da bird in da pare tree. Ah fix it las nite wit some dirty rice. Boy it wuz good, yeah. Ah don't tink da pare tree gon grow in da swamp, so, me, ah swap it faw a satsuma.

Day 2

Dear Boudreaux, Yo letta say dat ya sant two turtle dove, but all ah got, me, wuz two scrawny lil pigeons. Annyhow, ah mix dem wit some andouille sausage an made some gumbo outa dem.

Day 3

Dear Boudreaux, How come you don't sand some crawfish, you? Ahm tired o' eatin' dem doggone lil birds, me. Ah gave two o' dem prissy Franch chickens, dere, ta Maree Trahan ova at Fourchon and fed da tird one ta my dog, Phideaux. Maree, hur, she needed some sparing pardnas faw hur fightin' roosta.

Day 4

Dear Boudreaux, Mon Dieux! Ah tought ah tolju no mo' friggin' birds! Dese fo', watchu call dem "callin' birds", dey made so much noise, dem, dat ya could hear dem all da way ta Point Au Chien. Ah used their necs faw my crab traps and fed da rast o' dem ta da gators.

Day 5

Dear Boudreaux, Ya finely sant someting useful, you. Ah sho like dem golden rings, me. Ah hock dem at da pawn shop in Thibodaux and got enuff money ta fix da shaft on my shrimp boat and buy a roun' o' drinks faw da girls at da Raisin' Cane Lounge. Merci Beaucoup!

Day 6

Dear Boudreaux, Couyon! Back ta dem birds, dere, you Cajun turkey, you. Po' egg suckin' Phideaux is scaired ta deat o' dem six geeses. He try ta eat dem eggs, and dey peck da heck outa his snout. Dey good at eatin' da cockroaches, dough. Ah jis might stuff one ' dem wit erster dressin' on Christmas Day.

Day 7

Dear Boudreaux, Ahm gon wring yo fool nec, you, da next time ah see ya. T-June, da mailman, him, he's reddy ta kill ya, too, yeah. Da crap from all doze birds is stinkin' up his mailboat and he's scaired dat somebody gonna slip on dat stuff and sue him good. Ah let dem saven swans loose ta swam in da bayou and some redneck duck huntas from Mississippi blasted dem outa da wata. Talk witchu somemo' tamorra, sha.

Day 8

Dear Boudreaux, Po' ole T-June. He hadta make teree trips on his mailboat ta deliva dem eight maids-a-milkin' and dere cows. One o' dem cows got spooked by da alligatas and almos tip ova da boat. Cot dawg, dat wuz close, yeah! Ah don't like dem shiftless maids, non, me. Ah tol dem ta git ta work guttin' fish and sweepin' da shack, but dey say dat it wudn't in dere contrack. Dey probly tink dey too good, dem, ta skin da nutrias ah caught las nite, yeah!

Day 9

Dear Boudreaux, Wat da heck ya tryin' ta do, you? T-June hadta borra da Lutcher Ferry ta carry dem jumpin' twits you call "Lords a Leapin'" across da bayou. Da minute dey got here dey wanted a tea break wit crumpets. Ah don't kno wat dat meen, me, but ah say, "Well, la de da. Ya goin' git Community coffee or nuttin'." Sha lawd, Boudreaux, wat ahm goin' feed all dem bozos. Dey too snooty faw fried nutria, and da cows, dem, dey done eat up all my turnip greens.

Day 10

Dear Boudreaux, You gotta be outa yo mind, you. If da mailman don't kill you, him, ya kin be sho ahma do it, me. Taday he deliva tan haf-neckid floozies from Bourbon Street. Dey say dat dey da "Ladies Dancin'" but dey sho don't act like no ladies in da front o' doze Limey twits, non. Dey almos lef afta one o' dem got bit by a wata moccasin ova by da outhouse. Ah hadta butcha two cows ta feed dem and den hadta git some toilet paper. Da Sears catalog wudn't good enuff faw doze hoity toity Lords' royal behinds, non!

Day 11

Dear Boudreaux, Ware you at, you? Cheerio and pip pip. Yo elavan pipers piping got here taday from da House o' Blues, sacand lining as dey got offa da boat. Ah fixed stuff goose and beef jumbalaya, and we havin' us a fais-do-do rat na. Our new mailman, he's passing hissef a good time, him, yeah, dancin' wit all dem floozies. Po' T-June, him, he jump offa da Sunshine Bridge yestiddy, screamin' ya neem all da way down. If ya git you a mysterious lookin' package in da mail das tickin', don't open it, non!

Day 12

Dear Boudreaux, Ah jis wanna letchu kno dat ahm not yo true luv no mo', me. Afta da fais-do-do, dere, ah spant da nite wit Jacques, da hed pipa. We done decided, us, dat we goin' open a restrunt and gentlemen's club on da bayou. Da floozies, 'scuse me, da ladies dancin' kin make twanny dolla faw a table dance, and de lords kin be waitas and valet pawk da boats. Since da maids don't have no mo' cows ta milk, ah treened dem ta git my crab traps, watch my trotlines, and run my shrimpin' bidness. We probly goin' gross a million dolla next year, us. So long, sha!

Logical Conclusion

Boudreaux realized that he wanted to get more out of life, so he decided to take some evening courses at the vo-tech school near his home. At his interview with the enrollment counselor, he was told to take courses in math, English, and logic.

"Logic? May wat's dat?" asked Boudreaux.

The counselor answered by saying, "Let me give you an example. Do you own a lawn mower?"

"Haw yeah!" replied Boudreaux. "One o' dem Lawn Boys, dere, sha, da top o' da line!"

"Then I have to assume, using logic, that you have a yard," said the counselor.

"Cooooot dawg, das rat, yeah!" exclaimed Boudreaux. "Ah got me a big, big yard."

"Logic also tells me," continued the counselor, "That since you have a yard, you live in a house and not an apartment."

"Chooo, you some good, you!" said Boudreaux with excitement.

"Furthermore, since you live in a house, logic dictates that you have a wife," said the counselor.

"Doggone, you rat agin, you! Ah been married, me, ta Chlotilde faw tirty years, dere," responded Boudreaux.

"Finally, since you have a wife, logically, I can assume that you are heterosexual," said the counselor.

"Talk abot!" replied Boudreaux. "Dis is da mos fascinatin' ting ah done aver heard o', me. Ah jis can't wait faw dat logic class ta start, non!"

Boudreaux is so happy and proud that a new world of logic will soon be opening up to him. As he walked back into the waiting room, he saw a guy sitting waiting for his interview.

The guy asked, "So what classes are you taking?"

"Mat, Anglish and logic!" responded Boudreaux proudly.

"Logic? What's that?" asked the guy.

"It ain't dat hawd, non," said Boudreaux. "Lemme show ya. You own a lawn mota, you?"

"No," answered the guy.

"No!" replied Boudreaux. "Den you mus be gay, you!"

Age Is Relative

T-Brud was helping Boudreaux celebrate his birthday at the Hubba Hubba. As usual, Boudreaux had to share his innermost thoughts on the subject at hand.

"May, age is a funny ting, yeah," commented Boudreaux.

"Watchu meen, it's funny?" asked T-Brud.

"It all da time chenge, dere, you kno, how you look at it," replied Boudreaux.

"Get me annuda Bud and 'spleen ta me watcha meen," said T-Brud.

"Okay, it's like dis," started Boudreaux. "Ya realize da only time in our life wen we like ta git old is wen we're lil kids? If ya less den tan years old, you so axcited abot aging dat you tink in fractions. 'How old you are?' 'Ahm fo' and a haf, me.' Ya nava tirty-six and a haf, butchu fo' and a haf goin' on five."

"Hummmmm, ah nava tought o' dat," admitted T-Brud.

"Den ya git in yo teens and dey can't hol you back," continued Boudreaux. "Ya jump ta da next numba. 'How old you are?' 'Ahm gon be sixteen, me.' Na, you could be twalve, butchu gon be sixteen, evantually."

"You kno you rat, yeah, Boudreaux," said T-Brud.

"And it git mo betta den dat, yeah, cuz da great day o' yo life finely come," said Boudreaux. "Das wen you become twanny-one. Even da word sound lika saramony! You BECOME twanny-one — aw yeah. Den ya turn tirty. Wat happened dere? It kinna make ya sound like some bad milk or someting. He TURNED, so we hadta tarow him out! Wat happened? You BECAME twanny-one, butcha TURNED tirty."

"Dat don't sound too good, non," remarked T-Brud as he guzzled his beer.

"Hey, Cap, give us a coupla mo' Buds faw me and da birtday boy, dere."

"You gon lemme finish you or wat?" asked Boudreaux.

"May yeah, go hed, you," replied T-Brud. "Ah jis can't take all dis deep level tinkin', dere, witout da beer."

"Okay, den ya PUSHING fawty and ya REACH fifty,"

explained Boudreaux. "Den ya MAKE IT ta sixty. By dis time you done built up so much speed dat you HIT saventy. Afta dat, it's a day by day ting. You HIT Wednesday, ya HIT Tursday, ya HIT Friday!"

"Ya got a lot mo' o' dis?" asked T-Brud. "Cuz ahm gittin' kinna tired, me."

"Aw, jis drink yo beer and shut up, you!" admonished Boudreaux as he went on. "Wen ya git inta yo eighties, ya HIT lunch, ya HIT 4:30. Sha lawd, my maw maw, dere, don't even buy some green bananas no mo', hur!"

"Das bad, yeah," commented T-Brud as he sipped slowly.

"Talk abot!" said Boudreaux. "And it don't even end dere, non. Cuz ya git inta yo nineties and ya start goin' backwards! 'Ah wuz JUST ninety-two, me.' Den a strenge ting start ta happen. If ya make it ova a hundred, you lika lil kid agin. 'Ahm a hundred and a haf.' Like ah sed, T-Brud, age is a funny ting, yeah!"

"Ah guess ya rat," answered T-Brud. "But dis ain't funny — it's yo roun', you!"

Politically Correct

Boudreaux and Kymon were sipping a few cold ones at the Hubba Hubba. Boudreaux began to get philosophical as he often did once he had a couple of beers "under his belt."

"Ya kno wat, Kymon?" asked Boudreaux.

"Non, wat?" replied Kymon.

"Ya gotta be so doggone careful abot watcha say ta dem wamans taday," said Boudreaux. "Dey so sansitive, dem!"

"Watchu meen?" inquired Kymon.

"Ya can't jis come out and tell dem da troot, non," answered Boudreaux. "Ya gotta suga coat arryting."

"Like wat?" questioned Kymon.

"Maaaaay, like ya don't daire tell a woman dat she's a bad cook, non," explained Boudreaux. "Aw non, ya gotta tell hur dat she's 'microwave compatible' or she gon hol it against ya faw da res o' ya life, yeah!"

"Hummmmm," said Kymon.

"And den, don't even tink abot tellin' hur dat she gain some weight, hur," said Boudreaux. "Sha lawd, non, ya gotta say dat she's a 'metabolic unda achieva!'"

"Chooooo!" responded Kymon.

"And if ya wanna let hur kno she's a flirt or a tease, dere," continued Boudreaux, "Ta be on da safe side, ya betta say dat she take part, hur, in 'artificial stimulation!'"

"Ga-lee!" exclaimed Kymon.

"And don't even mantion da fac dat she got on too much jewelry, hur," said Boudreaux. "Haw non! You on much mo safa ground, dere, if ya jis say dat she's 'metallically overburdened'!"

"Pooooo! Ahm so glad ahma beer drinka, me, and not a macrow cuz ah can't keep up wit all dis," admitted Kymon shaking his head. "Ahd be in da dog house all da time faw sho, me!"

"Dem wamans, dey done come a long way, yeah, Kymon!" said Boudreaux. "But ah sho don't know ware dey goin'!"

The Trouble With Words

Boudreaux and Kymon were fishing in Catfish Lake below Golden Meadow early one morning. The speckled trout were only biting occasionally so they had an opportunity to talk.

"You kno wat, you?" asked Boudreaux.

"Wat?" asked Kymon.

"Dem doggone oxygen morons really confuse me, yeah!" replied Boudreaux.

"Shaaaaa! Ya mean oxy-morons don'tcha?" inquired Kymon.

"Yeah! Yeah! Das wat ah sed, me, dem oxygen morons!" answered Boudreaux.

"Annyhow, wat abot'em?" asked Kymon.

"Dey so stoopid, dem," said Boudreaux. "Dey don't make no sanse atall. Tings like 'act naturally', 'found missin', 'good grief', 'almos exactly', alone tagetta'."

"Das confusin' alrat," said Kymon. "But dey not da mos worstest ones, non."

"Watchu meen?" asked Boudreaux.

"Well, dere's 'small crowd', 'taped live', 'clearly misundastood', 'pretty ugly', and 'exact estimate'," answered Kymon.

"Cot dawg, life wuz a hol lot simpla, yeah, wen da Andy Griffith Sho wuz on da talavision," remarked Boudreaux. "It's planny, planny complicated na, dough."

"Well, ta tellya da.....whooooo!" yelled Kymon as he jerked his line. "Ah tink ah got me two spacks on my shad rig, dere!"

Deep Thoughts

Boudreaux and Shawee were at a picnic for the Fourth of July. Sitting in the shade of the trees, they were sipping a few brews and sharing some thoughts.

"Ya kno, Shawee, ah been tinkin', me," said Boudreaux.

"Aw lawd, here we go!" moaned Shawee. "Can'tchu jis drink ya beer and pass a good time, you?"

"Yabbut dese tings bodda me a lot, yeah," replied Boudreaux.

"Ah guess ah can't stop ya so ya mite as well go hed and tel me," countered Shawee with disgust.

"Lemme axe ya dis, 'if ya choke a smurf, wat color he gon turn, him?'" asked Boudreaux.

"DIS is wat's boddering you?" asked Shawee with amazement.

"May it kinna make ya wunda, huh?" responded Boudreaux.

"And how come dey sterilize da needles, dere, for letal injections?" questioned Boudreaux.

"Boudreaux, ya gotta git yosef a life or quit drinkin' beer, one or da udda!" commented Shawee.

"And den, wen cumpnies ship styrofoam, dere, wat dey pack it in?" continued Boudreaux.

"Sha lawd, dat teree laigged race don't look bad rat na, non!" said Shawee.

"And wat abot dis, how come wen it reens, dere, da sheep don't shrink?" asked Boudreaux in a concerned tone of voice.

"All ah kin say, me, is dat wen Miss Mawgret wuz carryin' you, she musta had a bad, bad fall, hur!" said Shawee as he picked up his beer and walked away.

Wishful Thinking

Boudreaux was walking on the beach at Grand Isle and found a bottle. He looked around and didn't see anyone so he opened it. A genie appeared and thanked him for letting her out.

The genie said, "I am so grateful to get out of that bottle that I will grant you any wish of your choice, but I can only grant one."

"Cooooot dawg, tank you, sha! Das so nice o' you!" said Boudreaux excitedly. "Lemme hava sacand, dere, so ah kin figa out wat ah want, me."

Boudreaux put all the wheels in motion trying to decide what he should ask for. Finally, he said, "Ya kno, beb, ah always wanted ta go ta Hawaii, me. But ah ain't nava been dere cuz ah can't fly. Dem arrpleens are too scairy faw me. Pooooo! On a boat, dere, ah git sick, sick, sick. So ah wish, me, faw a road ta be built from here ta Hawaii."

The genie thought for a minute and said, "No, I don't think I can do that. Just think of all the work involved. Consider all the piling needed to hold up a highway and how deep they would have to go to reach the bottom of the ocean. Imagine, too, all the concrete that would be needed. No, that's just too much to ask. I'm sorry but you'll have to reconsider and think of something else."

Boudreaux thought for a few minutes and then told the genie, "Dere's one udda ting ah all da time wanted, me. Ah wanna be able ta undastan wamans — wat make dem laff and cry, why dey so tampamantal, dem, how come dey so hawd ta git along wit, wen dey want attantion and wen dey don't. Ya kno, kinna like wat make'm tick."

The genie thought for a few minutes and said, "So, you want two lanes or four?"

You just might be a Cajun if.....

You have a "parrain" instead of a Godfather and "nan-nan" instead of a Godmother.

Your name ends in "eaux" or "oux".

Some words you'll probably never hear a Cajun say.....

"Dey sho ain't got enuff places ta gamble aroun' here, non."

"Ahm sho glad dey cut out all dem doggone church fairs, me."

Chapter 9

Boudreaux On Relationships

Binding Love

Boudreaux and Chlotilde were sitting on the front porch swing. "Oh Boudreaux, don'tcha luv me no mo', beb?" asked Chlotilde. "Haw yeah!" responded Boudreaux very quickly. "How come you axe someting so stoopid like dat?"

"Cuz ya nava tell me datcha do!" replied Chlotilde.

"Look," said Boudreaux. "On da day we wuz married, dere, ah tolju ah luv ya. If anyting chenge, ahm goin' letchu kno!"

All In The Family

All the good Catholics along the bayou go to church every Sunday morning. Before Mass begins, these friendly Cajuns sit in the pews and exchange pleasantries about family, work and life in general.

Suddenly, one Sunday, Satan appeared at the altar. Everyone began screaming and running for the front entrance, trampling each other in their determined effort to get away from Evil Incarnate. Soon, everyone was evacuated from the church except Boudreaux who was sitting calmly in his pew, seemingly oblivious to the fact that God's ultimate enemy was in his presence.

This confuses Satan a bit. He walked up to Boudreaux and said, "Hey, don't you know who I am?"

"Haw, yeah. Ah sho do, me. You da devil, you,"

"Well, aren't you afraid of me?" asked the devil.

"Pooooo, ah-guess-not, " answered Boudreaux.

"And why aren't you afraid of me?" inquired satan who was more than just a little perturbed at this point.

"Cuz, me dere, ah been married ta ya sista faw tirty years!" explained Boudreaux.

Extended Anniversary

Boudreaux and Kymon were having a few cold ones at the Hubba Hubba.

"Cot dawg, time sho fly by, yeah!" exclaimed Boudreaux.

"Watchu meen?" asked Kymon.

"Maaaaay, next munt it goin' be fawty years dat me and Chlotilde been married, us," said Boudreaux as he sipped his brew. "Sha, lawd, it look like it wuz only yestiddy dat we got hitched up."

"Das nice, yeah, but ya tought abot wat you goin'git hur faw hur present?" inquired Kymon.

"Haw yeah!" answered Boudreaux. "Ahm goin' take hur ta Hawaii, me!"

"Chooooo, dat's someting, dere! Das real nice. But watchu goin' do ta top dat faw ya fiftieth anniversary?" questioned Kymon.

"May ahm goin' go pick hur up!" exclaimed Boudreaux as he ordered another round.

For Whom The Man Wails

A man was reared in Cajun country, but had been living out of state for many years. On one of his infrequent visits, he stopped by the cemetery to place some flowers on the grave of his dearly departed mother. As he started back toward his car, his attention was diverted to another man kneeling at a grave. It was ole Boudreaux. He seemed to be praying with great intensity and kept repeating, "Why didja hafta ta die? Why didja hafta die? Why didja hafta die? Why didja hafta die?"

The man approached him and said, "Sir, I don't want to interfere with your private grief, but this demonstration of pain is more than I've ever seen before. For whom do you mourn so deeply? A child? A parent? A wife?

"Aw non," said Boudreaux somberly, "My wife's furst husbun!"

Every Dog Has His Day

Boudreaux and Chlotilde were in a terrible car accident, and Chlotilde's face was burned very badly. The doctor informed Boudreaux that, in order to do plastic surgery, he would need a donor since he could not use skin from the patient. Boudreaux volunteered some of his skin but the only place suitable for the doctor was from his buttocks. Boudreaux requested that no one, not even Chlotilde, be told of this since it was such a delicate matter.

After the surgery was completed, everyone was astounded at Chlotilde's new beauty. It was unbelievable how beautiful she was. All her friends and relatives just ranted and raved at her appearance.

Chlotilde was alone with Boudreaux one day and wanted to express her thanks and appreciation for what he had done for her. She said, "Beb, ah jis wanna tank ya faw watcha did faw me. Na ah kno how mucha luv me. Dere ain't no way ah kin aver repay you."

"Don't worry yosef ta deat abot dat, sha," said Boudreaux. "Ahm goin' git planny tanks, me, arry time yo mama come ova here and give ya a kiss on da cheek!"

For Better Or For Worse

Boudreaux and T-Brud were at the Hubba Hubba engaged in one of their favorite pastimes. After several hours of guzzling the liquid equivalent of barley and hops, they began discussing some of the great tragedies in life.

"Sha lawd, Boudreaux," said a reflective T-Brud, "Losing a wife gotta be hawd, yeah."

"Huh, das faw sho," commented Boudreaux. "Ah kno faw me, dere, it's almos impossible!"

Not Out of The Woods

Boudreaux feared Chlotilde was having an affair and he was very distraught. So he went out and purchased a handgun in the event his investigative findings proved true. In an attempt to confirm his suspicions, he decided to come home in mid-afternoon to check on Chlotilde. Much to his shock and dismay, he found her in bed with the mailman. Boudreaux was so despondent that he held the gun to his head and vowed to shoot himself. Chlotilde jumped out of bed and began begging and pleading with him not to pull the trigger. Hysterical at this point, Boudreaux yelled at Chlotilde, "Ya may as well shut up, you, cuz you next, yeah!"

Four Letter Words

Boudreaux and Chlotilde had just gotten married and were on their honeymoon. After four days, Chlotilde called her mama to come and get her.

"Mama, ya gotta come git me!" cried Chlotilde frantically. "Ah jis can't live wit Boudreaux no mo'. All he do, him, is use dem fo' letta words at me!"

"Wat kinna fo' letta words you talkin' bot, beb?" asked her mother.

"Ah can't tellya on da talafoam! Jis come git me!" pleaded Chlotilde.

Chlotilde's mother hurriedly drove to the honeymoon site. Upon arriving, she asked, "May wat dat man's tellin' ya dem dirty fo' letta words faw, sha? Wat kinna tings he's tellin' ya annyhow?"

"Aw mama, ahm so asheem ta repeat dem but faw you ah will. He keep tellin' me dat ah needa cook, wash and iron!"

Starting From Scratch

Boudreaux and Chlotilde were at Mass one Sunday morning. Instead of the usual homily, a married couple from another church parish was explaining all about a Marriage Encounter Weekend occurring in a few weeks. They were hoping to recruit some couples to attend.

In their talk, they used the analogy of an automobile and brought out how preventive maintenance, like changing the oil and rotating the tires, keeps the car in good operating condition.

They said that a Marriage Encounter Weekend did the same thing for a marriage — it was like a tune-up for the marriage.

Boudreaux leaned over to Chlotilde and whispered, "Oh beb, afta fifty-six years o' marriage, dere, it ain't a tune-up ah need, me, it's a new engine!"

Nothing But The Truth

Boudreaux and Chlotilde were sitting on their front porch swing reflecting on their many years of married life. The discussion finally reached the topic of faithfulness.

"Ya kno, beb, afta fifty years o' being hitched up wit you, dere, ah ain't nava been unfateful, non, me," said Boudreaux proudly. "How bot you, sha?"

"Ahm so asheem, me, but ah gotta tellya da troot. Ah been unfateful ta ya teree times," responded a hesitant Chlotilde.

Needless to say Boudreaux was devastated and even speechless for a moment. After a while, though, he got the courage to ask, "How couldja do dat ta me? And wit who?"

"Well, da furst time wuz wen ya lost yo job," explained Chlotilde, "And got in dat real bad caw wreck on da way hume. All yo front teet wuz knocked out and ya needed ta have a permanent bridge put it. Dat coss a lot o' money, yeah, and da dannis bill wuz high, high, high. Dere wuz no way we could pay dat wit you losing yo job and all. So dat's how ah took care o' da bill wit da dannis."

"Well den, wat wuz da sacand time?" questioned Boudreaux.

"You remamba wen ya had dat gall bladda okeration, dere?" asked Chlotilde.

"Do-ah-remamba-me?" retorted Boudreaux. "Pooooo, dat wuz some o' da most worstest peen ah nava did have, me!"

"Well, da hospital bill wuz so high, dere, dat we woulda nava been able ta pay it. Weeda nava got outa deat, us," said a sorrowful Chlotilde. "So, me, ah call da hed man at da hospital ta see if we could work someting out — and we sho did."

"Sha lawd, ahm so hurt, me!" said Boudreaux. "Den wat wuz da tird time?"

"Remamba da time you wuz runnin' faw da office o' Justice o' da Peace?" asked Chlotilde.

"Haaaaaw yeah!" replied Boudreaux, "Like it wuz yestiddy."

"And you fine out a coupla days, dere, rat befo' da elaction dat ya needed abot anudda two hundred and fifty votes ta win?" continued Chlotilde.

"Ah sho do," answered Boudreaux.

"Well, dat wuz da tird time!" confessed Chlotilde.

The Spirit Is Willing.....

Boudreaux and Chlotilde were newlyweds and, as a penance, vowed not to make love during Lent. One day Chlotilde bent over to pick up a potato that had fallen on the floor. The temptation was too great for Boudreaux to resist. They made love right on the spot.

Feeling guilty because he had broken his resolution, he went to confession. After listening to Boudreaux's contrite admission, the priest said, "Don't worry my son. God loves you and forgives you."

"Please don't kick us outa da church!" pleaded Boudreaux.

"Of course not, my son," replied the priest. "Why would you think we sould do that?"

"Maaaaay, cuz dey kick us outa da Winn-Dixie!" explained Boudreaux.

Not Getting Your Money's Worth

Boudreaux went to a lingerie shop to buy a gift for Chlotilde. It was their fortieth wedding anniversary, and he wanted to get something special. After explaining this to the sales lady, she showed him a cute teddy.

Boudreaux looked it over and said, "May, dat's real nice yeah, sha. How much it coss?"

"Only $50.00," said the sales lady.

"Beb, ya got anudda outfit, someting maybe a lil bit mo' sheer den dis?" asked Boudreaux.

"Yes, of course we do," said the lady. She retreated to the back of the store and returned with a teddy considerably thinner than the first one.

"How much faw dat one?" inquired Boudreaux.

"Only $100.00," replied the sales lady.

"Dat's real nice, too, yeah," said Boudreaux. "But ahm lookin' faw someting mo sheerer den dat, even."

"I think I know what you want, sir," said the lady. "I'll be right back." She again went to the back of the store bringing one out which was virtually transparent.

"Das mo like it," said Boudreaux. "Wat's da price on dis one?"

"$200.00," said the lady.

"Ahma take it," said Boudreaux. "Go hed and wrap it up, sha."

Boudreaux could hardly wait to see Chlotilde in her new negligee. He gave her the gift and asked her to try it on. Chlotilde went in the bedroom, opened the gift and was amazed at how thin the teddy was. She said to herself, "Dat ole goat bought me dis tin, tin gown. It's so tin dat he ain't even goin' kno whetta ahm waring it or not." So she took off all her clothes and didn't even put the teddy on. She walked back into the family room totally nude to model her "new gown" for Boudreaux.

Boudreaux looked at Chlotilde and said, "Cooooot dawg, you sho look good in dat gown, yeah, Chlotilde! But faw two hundred dolla, you woulda tought dat dey coulda iron all da wrinkles outa dere!"

What's Good For The Goose.....

An escaped convict broke into Boudreaux's house one night and tied up both him and Chlotilde. They had been asleep in the bedroom. As soon as he had the chance, Boudreaux turned to Chlotilde who was tied up on the bed in a skimpy nightgown and whispered, "Oh beb, dis guy probly ain't seen a woman in a long, long time, non. Jis cooperate wit anyting he want. Even if he wanna have sax witchu, jis go along wit it and pretand dat you like it. Our lives might depand on it, yeah!"

"Boudreaux," said Chlotilde spitting out the gag, "Ahm sho' glad you feel dat way, sha, cuz he jis tolme dat he tink you kinna cute!"

Part Time Lover

Boudreaux and Chlotilde had been married for just a few years, yet their marriage was filled with constant bickering and arguments. They had been at each other's throats for some time and felt that the only way to save their marriage was to seek counseling.

When they arrived at the counselor's office, he immediately opened the floor for discussion by asking, "What seems to be the problem?"

Boudreaux just put his head in his hands and remained silent. Not so Chlotilde. She began talking incessantly describing all the problems with their marriage. She claimed that Boudreaux was insensitive, lacked romance and passion, and spent entirely too much time with his "podnas" at the Hubba Hubba.

Without uttering a word, the counselor walked towards Chlotilde, grabbed her by the shoulders and kissed her passionately on the lips. She was speechless! The marriage counselor looked over at Boudreaux who simply stared in disbelief. He said to Boudreaux, "Your wife needs that at least twice a week!"

Boudreaux scratched his head and replied, "Ah guess ah could bring hur in on Chewsdays and Tursdays."

Love Him To Death

Boudreaux wasn't feeling well so he visited Dr. Fontenot for a checkup. The doctor broke the bad news to him. Boudreaux had only twenty-four hours to live. He hurried home to break the news to Chlotilde. They cried for a long while and tried to console each other.

Boudreaux composed himself long enough to ask, "Oh beb, since ah got me only twanny-fo' hours ta live, dere, you tink we could have sax?"

"Aw may yeah, sha," replied Chlotilde. "You ain't even gotta axe."

Four hours later they were lying in bed and Boudreaux turned to Chlotilde and said, "You kno ah only got me twanny mo' hour ta live, dere. You tink we could have sax agin?"

"Anyting faw you, beb, cuz ya kno how much ah luv ya," answered Chlotilde.

Another eight hours passed and she had fallen asleep from exhaustion. Boudreaux tapped her on the shoulder and asked, "Oh Chlo, ya kno ah only got me twalve mo hours lef, dere, how bot agin faw ole time sake, dere, huh?"

By this time Chlotilde was getting a little annoyed, but she reluctantly agreed.

After they finished she went back to sleep. Four hours later Boudreaux tapped her on the shoulder again and said, "Oh beb, ah sho hate ta keep bodderin' you, yeah, butcha kno ah only got me eight hours befo' ah die. Kin we do it one mo' time?"

Chlotilde turned to Boudreaux with a grimace on her face and said, "Lemme tellya someting, sha. You ain't gotta git up in da mornin', you, but ah do, me!"

That's What Friends Are For

Ages ago Boudreaux and Cowan decided to go out West. They were in a covered wagon but somehow got separated from the rest of the wagon train. Cowan was driving while Boudreaux was relaxing in the back. Suddenly, and without warning, Cowan heard a blood-curdling yell from Boudreaux.

"Wat's da matta back, dere?" inquired Cowan.

"Chooooo, dey gotta whole buncha Injuns on hosses back here chasin' us!" exclaimed Boudreaux.

"May how big are dey, Boudreaux?" asked Cowan.

Holding his thumb and finger about two inches apart, he said, "Dey only abot dis big!"

"Aw, das okay. Jis be sho ta tell me wen dey git bigga, dough," said Cowan.

About ten minutes later Cowan yelled out to Boudreaux, "Oh Boudreaux, how big dem Injuns is na?"

"Huh, dey abot teree feet tall, dem," replied Boudreaux.

"Das still okay. We not in no deenger yet, non," assured Cowan.

A short while later Cowan once again calls out, "Oh Boudreaux, how big is dem Injuns?"

"Sha lawd," shouted Boudreaux, "Dey as big as me and you!"

"Well den shoot'm!" screamed Cowan. "Shoot'm!"

"May Cowan, ah can't shoot'm," replied Boudreaux holding his thumb and two fingers inches apart. "Ah been knowin'em arry since dey wuz dis big, me!"

Home For The Holidays

Boudreaux called his son who was living in New York and said, "Junya, ah got someting ta tellya but ah don't wanna talk abot it afta, non. Ahm jis tellin' you cuz you my oldest and ah tought ya oughta kno. Ah done made up my mind, me, ahm leaving yo mama."

"You mean you divorcing mama?" asked a shocked Junya.

"Das rat, boy," replied Boudreaux.

"May wat happened, poppa?" inquired Junya.

"Ah alreddy tolju, ah don't wanna talk abot it," said Boudreaux emphatically. "Ah done made up my mind, me, and dat's dat."

"But, Poppa, you don't decide to divorce mama jis like dat afta fifty-fo' years tagetta," explained Junya. "Wat happened?"

"It's way too peenful faw me ta talk abot it," responded Boudreaux. "Ah jis called you cuz you my boy and ah tought you oughta kno. Ah don't wanna git inta it annymo' den dis. You kin call yo sista and tell hur. Das goin' spare me da peen."

"But wares mama?" asked Junya. "Kin ah talk wit hur?"

"Ah don't wanchu ta say nuttin' ta yo mama abot dis, non," said Boudreaux, "Cuz ah ain't tole hur yet. You kin bleeve me wen ah say dat it ain't been easy, non. Ah done look at dis ting, me, from arry side, dere, and ah come up wit dis decision. Ah got, me, a meetin' wit da lawya da day afta tamorra."

"Poppa, pleez don't do nuttin' stoopid," pleaded Junya. "Ahm goin' take da furst pleen down. Jis promise me datchu ain't goin' do nuttin' til ah git dere."

"May okay, ahma do dat faw ya," said Boudreaux. "Next week is Christmas, dere, and ahm goin' hold off seeing da lawya til afta dat. Call yo sista in New Jersey and give hur da news. Ah jis can't talk abot it no mo', me."

A half hour later Boudreaux received a call from his daughter, Colinda. She said that she and Junya were able to get tickets and would be home day after tomorrow.

"Junya tol me datchu din wanna talk abot it on da talafoam and dat's okay faw na," said Colinda. "Jis promise me datchu ain't goin' do nuttin' til we bote git dere, Poppa."

"Don'tchu worry, sha, ah promise," said Boudreaux.

After hanging up the phone, Boudreaux turned to Chlotilde and said, "Well, beb, it worked dis time but wat we goin' do da next time ta git dem ta come hume faw da holidays!"

Mistaken Identity

"Hey Boudreaux, you batta gitcha sef some new blinds on ya bedroom winda, yeah," cautioned T-Boy.

"May how come?" asked Boudreaux.

"Cuz las Tursday nite wen ah passed by ya house ah could see da shadow on da wall o' you and Chlotilde makin' love," responded T-Boy.

"You so stoopid, you," replied Boudreaux. "You don't even kno watchu talkin' abot cuz ah wudn't even hume las Tursday!"

The Truth Prevails

Two Texiens boarded a flight from Houston for New Orleans. One sat in the window seat, the other in the middle seat. Just before takeoff, a little Cajun, Boudreaux, got on and took the aisle seat next to the Texiens. He kicked off his shoes, wiggled his toes and was settling in when the Texien in the window seat said, "I think I'll go up and get myself a coke, partner."

"Maaaaay, jis stay rat dere, sha," said Boudreaux. "Ahma be glad ta go git it faw ya."

While he was gone, the Texien picked up one of Boudreaux's shoes and spit in it. When Boudreaux returned with the coke, the other Texien said, "That looks mighty good, partner. I wouldn't mind having one of those, too."

"Dat ain't no prablum, non," replied Boudreaux. "Sheeeee, ahma git dat ting faw ya in a flash, me."

While he was gone the Texien picked up the other shoe and spit in it. Boudreaux returned with the coke, and they all sat back and enjoyed the short flight into New Orleans. As the plane was landing, Boudreaux slipped his feet into his shoes and knew immediately what had happened.

"How long is dis gon go on, huh?" asked Boudreaux in disgust. "All dese hard feelin's dere, dis bad blood, da hatred batween da Cajuns and da Texiens, dis spittin' in da shoes and da peeing in da cokes?"

Man's Best Friend

When Boudreaux was courting Chlotilde, he was delighted to finally be asked home to meet her parents. Naturally he was quite nervous about the meeting. By the time he arrived at the doorstep, he was in a state of gastric distress. The problem developed into one of acute flatulence, gas from the bowels. Halfway through the bread pudding, Boudreaux realized he couldn't hold it in one second longer without exploding. So he let a little gas escape.

"Phideaux!" shouted Chlotilde's mother to the family dog lying at Boudreaux's feet.

Relieved at the dog having been blamed, Boudreaux let another, slightly larger one go.

"Phideaux!" the mother called out sharply.

"Chooooo! Ah got it made, me," thought Boudreaux to himself. "One mo' and ahma feel good, good."

So he let loose a really big one.

"Phideaux!" shrieked the mother. "Git ova here, boy, befo' he crap all ova you!"

Not Rocket Science

"Ah done had it wit Chlotilde, me," said Boudreaux to Kymon as they were having a beer. "Ahm goin' see me a lawya abot a divorce."

"Ahm sho sorry ta hear dat, yeah," commented Kymon. "But kin ah axe ya why?"

"Cuz ah found some birt control pills in hur purse," explained Boudreaux. "Das why!"

"Look Boudreaux," said Kymon, "Ah kno you a good Catlic and all, but ah jis can't see ya leavin' Chlotilde faw wat da church, dere, say is a sin."

"It ain't jis dat, non," said Boudreaux. "Da prablum is dat ah had me one o' dem vasectomies ova five years ago, dere!"

Getting The Bugs Out

Boudreaux and Chlotilde had reservations at the Watergate Hotel in Washington, D.C. for their honeymoon. Chlotilde was a bit concerned on their arrival.

"May wat if dis place is still bugged, Boudreaux?" asked Chlotilde.

"Aw, don'tcha worry bot nuttin', beb," comforted Boudreaux. "Ahma look all aroun', me, ta see if dey still got one o' dem bugs, dere."

He looked behind the drapes, behind the pictures and under the rug.

"Aha!" shouted Boudreaux excitedly. "Ah found dat son-a-ba-gun!"

Under the rug was a disc with four screws. He got out his filet knife, unscrewed the screws, and threw them and the disc out the window.

The next morning, the hotel manager nervously asked the newlyweds, "How was your room? How was the service? How was your stay at the Watergate Hotel?"

"May how come ya askin' us all dese questions, you?" inquired Boudreaux.

"Because the room UNDER yours complained of the chandelier falling on them," replied the manager.

Share And Share Alike

A young man saw an elderly couple, Boudreaux and Chlotilde, sitting down to lunch at McDonald's. He noticed that they had ordered one meal and an extra drink cup. As he watched, Boudreaux carefully divided the hamburger in half, then counted out the fries — one for him, one for her — until each had half of them. Then he poured half of the soft drink into the extra cup and put that in front of Chlotilde. Boudreaux then began to eat, and Chlotilde sat watching, with her hands folded in her lap.

"Would you please allow me to buy another meal for you so that you don't have to split it?" asked the young man.

"Aw non," replied Boudreaux. "We been hitched up us faw fifty years na and arrying done all da time been shair and shair alike wit us, fifty-fifty, dere."

"Well, aren't you going to eat?" the young man asked Chlotilde.

"Not yet, sha," answered Chlotilde. "It's his turn wit da teet!"

Or What?

Boudreaux and Shawee were discussing what they would do upon retirement. Boudreaux said he had a lot of hobbies, including golf, and finding things to do would not be a problem. Shawee, however, was very concerned because he had none. The thought of retirement with nothing to do bothered him very much.

"Maaaaay, jis go visit yo kids, you," suggested Boudreaux.

"Ah guess ah could do dat, but sance ah only got two kids, me, dat wouldn't take too long, non," said Shawee. "But ah could buy me one o' dem mota humes and go visit my bruddas and my sistas a coupla weeks each. Dat would take abot a year."

"Abot a year?" questioned Boudreaux.

"Haw yeah," answered Shawee. "Ahm one o' eighteen chiren in da famly."

"Sha lawd! Eighteen chiren!" exclaimed Boudreaux. "Yo papa, dere, he din have no hobbies him edda, huh?"

"Don't be no smart alec, non, you," said Shawee. "Da prablum wuz my mama wuz hawd o' hearin', hur," explained Shawee.

126

"Hawd o' hearin'?" asked a puzzled Boudreaux.

"Das rat," said Shawee. "Arry nite, dere, wen mama and papa would go ta bed, papa would axe, 'ya wanna go ta sleep or wat?' and mama would say, 'wat?'"

Inseparable

Boudreaux and Chlotilde were dating and on one occasion they were embracing passionately in the front seat of his car.

"Wanna go in da back seat, beb?" asked Chlotilde.

"Aw non!" responded Boudreaux immediately.

A few minutes later when things became more passionate she asked, "Na ya wanna go in da back seat?"

"May non, sha!" answered Boudreaux. "Ah wanna stay in da front seat witchu!"

No Big Mystery

"Oh beb, lemme axe ya someting, dere," said Boudreaux. "Watcha been doin' wit all da grocery money dat ah been givin' ya arry munt?"

"Huh, dat ain't no big mystery, non," responded Chlotilde. "Jis turn sideways, dere, and look in da mirra, sha!"

Open Minded

"Hey Cowan," said Boudreaux, "It's my ole lady's birtday, dere, taday. Chlotilde's fifty-teree, hur."

"May das nice," responded Cowan. "Watcha gittin' faw hur?"

"Ah don't kno. How much ya offrin'?" laughed Boudreaux.

No Big Mystery

You just might be a Cajun if.....

After a hurricane you pray for a little rain shower to wash the mud off of the grass.

You've gone to confession and admitted that you've coveted a shrimp boat.

Some words you'll probably
never hear a Cajun say.....

"Ah wish we had Lent teree or fo' times a year, us."

"Ah wish ah din havta eat all dat seafood on Fridays in Lent, me."

Chapter 10

Boudreaux On Spiritual Matters

The Here After

"Oh Boudreaux, do ya aver tink abot da hereafta?" asked T-Brud.

"Haw yeah," replied Boudreaux. "Arrytime ah go inta da kitchen, dere, and ah open da ice box, den ah open da freeza and look inside and finely ah walk aroun' inside da pantry. Ah scratch my haid den axe mysef, 'may wat ahma here afta?'"

Name That Tune

A German, an Englishman, and a Cajun, Boudreaux, were greeted by St. Peter at the Pearly Gates.

Said St. Peter to the trio, "In order to enter heaven you must correctly answer one question. And here it is. How many "L's" are there in the song 'Here Comes The Bride'?"

"None," responded the German.

"Correct," said St. Peter.

"None," replied the Englishman.

"Correct as well," smiled St. Peter.

"Haw non," chimed Boudreaux. "Dey got foteen in dere!" exclaimed Boudreaux.

"Fourteen?" asked a puzzled St. Peter. "How in the world did you come up with that number?"

"Maaaaay, dat's simple. La la la la, la la la la ....!" exclaimed a triumphant Boudreaux.

Holding On Til The End

Boudreaux, Shawee and Cowan were engaged in their favorite pastime at the Hubba Hubba. When the bartender brought another round of Bud, he posed a question to them.

"Lemme axe yall dis, fellas," said the bartender. "Wen you die, dere, and dey putcha in yo casket and all ya frans and famly is in mournin' and lookin' ova ya, wat woodja wanna hear dem say abotcha?"

"Chooooo, dat's easy," said Shawee, "Ah would jis like dem ta say dat ah wuz da bestess hunta and fishaman in da hol Sot Lafooche area and dat ah luved da outdoors."

"Not me," countered Cowan. "Ah would like ta hear dem say dat ah wuz a wundaful husbun and famly man. Ah sho luv my wife and my kids, me, and ah all da time put dem furst."

"How bot you, Boudreaux?" quizzed the bartender. "Watcha want dem ta say abotchu?"

"Me dere, da only ting ah wanna hear dem say is, 'sha lawd, ah tink he's moving!'" exclaimed Boudreaux.

Unorthodox Farmer

Boudreaux and T-Brud were engaged in conversation one Sunday morning while having coffee at the kitchen table. Boudreaux had just returned from 9 o'clock Mass (Church) which prompted T-Brud to make a comment.

"Cot dawg, Boudreaux, you sho are religious, you. Wuz ya always dat way?"

"Haw non," responded Boudreaux quickly, "Ah come a long way, me. Ah kin remamba, dere, wen ah wuz a young man in my early twenties, da extant o' my religion wuz ta go out on Sadday nite and sow my wild oats and den go ta church on Sunday mornin' and pray faw a crop failure!"

Crisis In The Gulf

Boudreaux had been going to Mass every day which prompted Kymon to discover what was the reason.

"Oh Boudreaux," said Kymon, "Ah see dat ya been goin' ta church arry day, dere. Ya ain't nava been dat religious befo'. Wat's goin' on witchu?"

"Well, ta tel da troot," answered Boudreaux, "Ah been watching da news arry night on da talavision. And dey say dat dere's some trouble wit us and Iraq. Dey keep talkin' abot Christ is in da gulf. Ah ain't no road skolla, me, but if he's dat close, den da end o' da world can't be too far away, non. So, me dere, ahm jis tryin' ta cova all da bases and git in all da points ah kin!"

Unholy Symptons

Boudreaux was talking with the priest after Mass one Sunday morning.

"Fadda, wat causes artritis? inquired Boudreaux.

"I'll tell you what!" answered the priest excitedly. "It's caused by loose living, being with cheap, wicked women, too much alcohol and a contempt for your fellow man!"

"Huh, ah'll be doggone, me," said a reflective Boudreaux.

The priest thought about what he had said and began to feel apologetic.

"I'm sorry, Boudreaux," said the priest, " I didn't mean to come on so strong and seem unsympathetic. Tell me, how long have you had arthritis?"

"Oh no, Fadda. Ah don't have it, me," responded Boudreaux. "Ah jis read in da paper dis mornin' dat da Pope got it."

Highway To Heaven

A visiting priest from an out of state diocese was in town to preach a one week mission. On the first morning, he stepped out of the rectory to mail a letter. Not knowing where the post office was, he stopped the first passerby to ask directions. It was Boudreaux, who explained that it was just a half mile down the bayou. The priest was very appreciative for the information and asked Boudreaux if he was coming to the mission tonight.

"Pooooo non," responded Boudreaux.

"Why not?" asked the priest.

"Cuz ah go ta church arry Sunday morning, me. Ah sho don't needa go arry nite during da week," explained Boudreaux.

"But if you come," continued the priest, "I'll show you how to get to heaven."

"Huh!   How ya goin' sho me how ta git ta heaven," said Boudreaux.   "You can't even fine da poss office, you!"

Heaven Can't Wait

Boudreaux and Chlotilde had been married for more than sixty years. They tragically passed away in a car accident. When they arrived at the Pearly Gates, St. Peter greeted them and said, "Welcome to heaven! Let me show you around."

St. Peter led them directly to the golf clubhouse where they found a lavish buffet with cuisine from around the world.

"Dis is good, good yeah," said Chlotilde," But da bote o' us, we only eat low fat and low cholestrol meals. Ya got summa doze?"

St. Peter smiled and said, "Forget that stuff! This is heaven! You'll never get fat or sick again!"

Next, Boudreaux and Chlotilde followed St. Peter to a beautiful house with a large new kitchen and great master bath suite — complete with a jacuzzi.   Chlotilde whispered to Boudreaux, "Caaaaaw! Dis is someting, huh beb? But don'tcha tink dat it's jis a lil bit too high class faw us?"

St. Peter, overhearing her, replied, "Don't worry about it. Remember, you're in heaven now. The house is yours and is absolutely free!"

Boudreaux suddenly began looking very solemn and depressed as St. Peter took them out to the porch overlooking the fairway of the fabulous golf course. He explained that a tee time was reserved for them everyday. He further explained that the course would change daily to replicate the greatest golf courses of the world. Today it's Pebble Beach, tomorrow St. Andrews.

"Pooooo, dat sho is purty, yeah!" commented Chlotilde. "But how much dem green fee gonna coss us?"

"Absolutely nothing. They, too, are free," replied St. Peter.

Boudreaux couldn't contain himself any longer. He shook his head and shouted at Chlotilde, "How come ya made us eat all dem doggone bran muffins arry day?   We coulda been here tan years ago, us!"

Not In That Number

The priest was giving his homily at Mass on the first Sunday of Lent. The sermon focused on repentance. Father forcefully brought out the point that this needed to be seriously considered because one day everyone in this parish was going to die.

Boudreaux was sitting in the first pew and began giggling. He could not restrain himself, and the giggling soon turned to laughter.

"Boudreaux!" said the priest, "What do you find so funny? Why are you laughing?"

"Cuz ahm not from dis parish, me," responded Boudreaux.

Why Didn't You Say So?

Boudreaux's dog, Phideaux, was hit and killed by a car. He was a great dog and very special to Boudreaux. He was a good friend and like a member of the family. Because of this close relationship, Boudreaux felt that he needed to do something exceptional for the deceased canine, so he went to see his Pastor to ask if something could be done.

"Oh Fadda," said Boudreaux, "My dog Phideaux was killed, and ah sho luved dat dog, yeah. Ah wuz jis wundring, me, if we could hava service faw him at church."

"Boudreaux, I'm shocked that you would even consider asking such a thing!" exclaimed the priest. "I'd never think of doing that but you might want to check with that off-the-wall church around the corner."

"Dat's a good idear, dere, Padre," said Boudreaux. "You tink it would help if ah offered dem a five hundred dolla donation?"

"Wait a minute, Boudreaux!" replied the priest. "Why didn't you say Phideaux was Catholic?"

Little Comfort

One of Boudreaux's uncles was a Catholic priest.   Father Boudreaux went to the hospital to visit one of his parishioners who was seriously ill.   Father sat at his bedside and talked even though the patient could not respond.   After a while, the parishioner scribbled a note with much difficulty and handed it to the priest. Wanting to do his priestly duties and comfort the patient, the good Father continued to talk and put the note in his coat pocket. Within minutes the patient died.   Father Boudreaux was extremely upset, so he didn't want to read the note at that time.

Two days later at the funeral, Father Boudreaux was eulogizing the deceased in his homily.   He shared with those in attendance that the very last act of the departed was to pass him a note.   He also said that he hadn't read it yet because he had been too upset. Instead, he invited a family member to come up and read it.   The relative took the folded note from Father, opened it and read, "HELP, FADDA! YA STAPPING ON MY OXYGEN LINE AND AH CAN'T BREADE!"

Holy Cut

Boudreaux went to Kymon's barber shop for a haircut.

"Gimme a good one, sha." said Boudreaux.   "Ahm goin' ta Rome ta see da Pope, me!"

"Couyon! You don't tink faw a sacand, dere, dat you goin' git ta see da Pope!" exclaimed Kymon.

"Maaaaay, ah don't see why not, me," said Boudreaux. "Ahma good Catlic and ahm comin' all da way from da bayou. Ah really bleeve he goin' see me, yeah."

Four weeks later Boudreaux returned to the barber shop for another haircut.

"You got ta see da Pope, you?" asked Kymon.

"Haw yeah!" said Boudreaux.

"May wat happened?" questioned Kymon excitedly.

"We wuz in St. Peter's Square, dere, ya kno, wit tousands and tousands o' people," said Boudreaux.   "Da Pope, him, he come out

136

on da balcony, give arrybody his blessin' and den start ta give his message. Den he spot me in da crowd and he stop and make a sign faw me ta come up dere wit him on da balcony."

"Coooot dawg!" said a wide-eyed Kymon. "Den wat happened?"

"Well, da security guards, dem, dey come git me and bring me wit him," replied Boudreaux.

"Sha lawd! Wat he hadta say ta you?" inquired Kymon.

"Aw, not too much," answered Boudreaux. "He jis wanna kno ware ah got, me, dis crappy lookin' harecut!"

The Wrong Conclusion

Boudreaux's daughter, Colinda, brought her fiancee home to meet him and Chlotilde. Boudreaux invited the young man, Pierre, under the carport for a beer.

"May, wat kinna plans ya got faw my daughta, dere, sha?" asked Boudreaux as he handed Pierre a Bud.

"I'm a scripture scholar, sir," answered Pierre.

"A scripcha skolla, huh," said Boudreaux. "Dat sound good, yeah, but how ya goin' have a nice house faw Colinda ta live in?"

"I will study hard," replied Pierre, "And God will provide for us."

"And how ya goin' buy hur a real nice engagement ring, dere?" questioned Boudreaux.

"I will be totally focused and concentrate on my studies," responded Pierre, "And God will provide for us."

"And chiren? How ya goin' support some chiren?" asked Boudreaux.

"Don't worry, sir, God will provide," responded Pierre confidently.

The conversation continued like this with Pierre insisting that God would provide each time Boudreaux asked a question.

Later that evening when Boudreaux and Chlotilde were alone, she asked, "May how it went wit Pierre, beb?"

"Well, sha, ah got some good news and some bad news," said Boudreaux. "Da bad news is dat he ain't got no job and no plans atall, him. But da good news is dat he tink ahm God, me!"

The Rest Of The Story

Boudreaux was reading Bible stories to his young son, Junya.

"Da man neemed Lot, dere, wuz warned ta take his wife and flee outa da city, but his wife, she look back, hur, and wuz turned ta salt," read Boudreaux.

"May wat happened ta da flea, Poppa?" asked Junya.

Long Winded

Boudreaux got dressed for church one Sunday morning. The priest began his homily during Mass and just kept on talking. The sermon went on endlessly until finally Boudreaux rose and started walking out.

The priest knew him so he called out, "Hey Boudreaux, where are you going?"

"Ahm goin' git me a harecut," answered Boudreaux.

"Well why didn't you get that before coming to church?" asked the priest.

"Cuz ah din need one den!" replied Boudreaux.

Holy Moley

Boudreaux walked into the ladies department at Dilliard's Department Store. He shyly went up to the lady behind the counter and said, "Ahm so haunt, me, but ah guess ah gotta do dis annyhow."

"How can I help you, sir?" asked the saleslady.

"Ah needa bra, me," said Boudreaux. "It's faw my wife Chlotilde's birtday."

"What type of bra would you like?" asked the clerk.

"Sha lawd, you mean dey got mo' den one kind o' dem ting?" responded Boudreaux. "Dat must be da secret dat Victoria got, dere, huh?"

"Look at these," said the saleslady as she showed him an endless stream of bras in every shape, size and material.

"Actually, even with all of this variety, there are really only three types of bras," explained the clerk.

"Pooooo! Tank God faw dat!" exclaimed Boudreaux. "May wat dey are, dem?"

"The Catholic type, the Salvation Army type and the Baptist type," replied the saleslady.

"May wat's da diffrence batween all o' dem?" asked a confused Boudreaux.

"It's all quite simple," answered the clerk. "The Catholic type supports the masses, the Salvation Army type lifts up the fallen and the Baptist type makes mountains out of mole hills."

"Den ya betta gimme teree o' dem Baptist kind, well," said Boudreaux.

Aim To Please

Sometime after Boudreaux died, his widow, Chlotilde, was finally able to speak about what a thoughtful and wonderful man her late husband had become.

"Boudreaux tought o' arryting," she told her friends. "Jis befo' he died, he called me ova ta his bedside and handed me teree anvelops. 'Beb,' he told me, 'ah done put all o' my las wishes in dese teree anvelops. Wen ahm dead, dere, ah wancha ta open dem and do 'zackly like ah wrote it down. Den ah kin rast in peace, me.'"

"What wuz in da furst anvelop?" asked Suzette.

"Da furst anvelop, dere, had five tousand dolla in it wit a note, 'pleez use dis money ta buy me a nice, nice coffin,'" replied Chlotilde. "So, me, ah bought'm a real good mahogany casket. Sha, dey don't come no betta den dat, non. Dey got a soft, soft lining on da inside, dere, so ah kno' faw a fac dat ole Boudreaux is rasting in peace, him."

"Da sacand anvelop," continued Chlotilde, "Had tan tousand dolla in it wit a note, 'pleez use dis faw a nice funral.' So me, dere, ah fix'm up wit a furst class funral and cook all o' his mos favorite foods. Cot dawg, dey had gumbo, potata salid, jumbalaya, crab fricasse, and crawfish etouffe. Faw dessert, ah made some apple pie, bouille, and faw sho', dem brownie dat he like so much. He woulda been gonflayed if heeda been dere, ah guarontee ya dat."

"And wat abot dat tird anvelop, dere?" inquired Suzette.

"Well, dat tird anvelop," said Chlotilde, "Had twanny-five tousand dolla in it wit a note, 'Pleez use dis money ta buy a nice stone.'

Holding her hand in the air and showing off her ten carat diamond ring, Chlotilde said, "May watchu tink abot my stone, sha?"

Learned That Lesson Well

Chlotilde passed away and the wake was being held at the local funeral home. As the pallbearers were carrying out the casket to put into the hearse, they accidentally bumped the coffin against the wall causing a tremendous jolt.

They heard a faint moan, and curiosity prompted them to open the casket. Much to their surprise and amazement, they found Chlotilde was actually alive.

She lived for ten more years and then died. The wake was again held at the same funeral parlor as before. Once again the pallbearers were carrying out the casket to the hearse in order to transport the body to the church. As they were walking, Boudreaux yelled, "Hey! Watch out faw dat wall, dere!"

Tough Choice

One day while Boudreaux was walking down the street, he was hit by a bus and died. His soul arrived in heaven where he was met by St. Peter himself.

"Welcome to heaven," said St. Peter. "Before you get settled in, though, it seems we have a minor problem. You see, strangely enough, we've never had a Cajun make it this far before, and we're really not sure what to do with you."

"May das no prablum, Pete," answered Boudreaux. "Jis lemme in, sha!"

"Well, I'd like to, but I have higher orders," replied St. Peter. "What we're going to do is, first, you'll have a day in hell and a day in heaven. Then you can choose which ever one you want to spend eternity in."

"Ta tellya da troot, Pete, ah tink ah done made up my mind already, me," said Boudreaux. "Ah radda stay rat here in heaven."

"Sorry, but we have rules," responded St. Peter.

And with that St. Peter put Boudreaux in an elevator and it went down, down, down to hell. The doors opened and he found himself stepping out onto the putting green of a beautiful golf course. In the distance was a country club and standing in front of him were all of his friends — fellow Cajuns he had worked with — and they were all dressed in tuxedos and cheering wildly for him. They ran up to Boudreaux, shook his hand, pat him on the back and talked about old times. They played a fantastic round of golf and that night went to the country club where he enjoyed a delicious steak and lobster dinner. He met the devil who was actually a really nice guy. Boudreaux had a great time telling Cajun jokes and dancing. He was having such a good time, that before he knew it, it was time to leave. Everybody shook his hand and waved good-bye as he stepped into the elevator.

The elevator went up, up, up and opened at the Pearly Gates where he found St. Peter waiting for him.

"Now, Boudreaux, it's time to spend a day in heaven," said St. Peter.

So he spent the next twenty-four hours lounging around on clouds, playing the harp and singing. He had a great time and, before he knew it, his twenty-four hours had passed. St. Peter came for him.

"So, Boudreaux, you've spent a day in hell and one in heaven," said St. Peter. "Now you must choose your eternity."

Boudreaux paused for a moment and then said, "Sha lawd, ah nava tought ahd say dis, me. Heaven, dere, wuz good, good, good yeah, but ta be honest witchu, ah tink ah had me a mo' batta time in hell."

"That's your choice and I'll honor it," said St. Peter. So he escorted Boudreaux to the elevator and again he went down, down, down — back to hell. When the doors of the elevator opened, he found himself standing in a desolate wasteland covered in garbage and filth. He saw his friends were dressed in rags and were picking up the garbage and putting it in sacks. The devil came to him and put his arm around him.

"Cooooot dawg, ah don't undastan dis, me!" said Boudreaux.

"Yestiddy, dere, ah wuz here and dere wuz a gulf course and country club. Ah wuz smackin' dem drives teree hundred yards down da fareway. We ate us some lobsta, danced and passed oursefs a good time. Na all dey got here is a wasteland wit garbage and all my frans, dem, dey boodayed. How kin dat be?"

The devil looked at Boudreaux, smiled and said, "Yesterday we were recruiting you, today you're on staff."

Religious Stamps

Boudreaux went to the post office to buy stamps for his Christmas cards.

"Uuuuuh, gimme a hundred stamp dere, pleez," said Boudreaux.

"What denomination?" asked the clerk.

"Sha lawd, ah can't bleeve we done come down ta dat, me," exclaimed Boudreaux. "Okay, den gimme fifty Baptist and fifty Catlic ones!"

The Numbers Game

Father June made reference to the ten commandments in his homily at Mass one Sunday morning. He asked if anyone could name them in any order. Boudreaux raised his hand.

"Great, Boudreaux!" said Father excitedly. "Go ahead."

"Maaaaay, teree, six, won, eight, fo', five, nine, two, tan and saven," said Boudreaux proudly.

Hairy Argument

Boudreaux's son, Junya, had just gotten his driving permit. He asked his father if they could discuss the use of the car.

Boudreaux said, "Ahma maka deal witchu, son. You bring up yo grades, study da Bible a lil bit and gitcha hare cut and we goin' talk abot it."

A month later Junya approached his father and again wanted to discuss the use of the car.

"Boy, ahm real prod o' you, yeah," said Boudreaux. "You done brought up ya grades, studied da Bible arry nite, but you din gitcha hare cut."

Junya thought a moment and then replied, "Poppa, ah been tinking a lot abot dat, me. Ya kno, dere, Samson had long hare, Moses had long hare, Noah had long hare, and even Jesus, he had long hare."

"Aw yeah, and dey walked arrywares dey went, too!" answered Boudreaux.

Answered Prayer

Boudreaux went on vacation in hill country and decided to skip Mass on Sunday to do some bear hunting. As he rounded the corner on a dangerous twist in the trail, he and a bear collided sending him and his rifle tumbling down the mountain. Before he knew it, his rifle went one way and he went the other, landing on a rock and breaking both legs. That was the good news.

The bad news was that the ferocious bear came charging at him from a distance and he couldn't move.

"Sha lawd, God," prayed Boudreaux, "Ahm so sorry, me, faw not goin' ta Mass dis mornin' ta come out here ta hunt. Pleez fogive me, God, and, cot dawg, if ah could have jis one wish, me, it would be faw you ta make a Christian outa dat bear dat's hedded rat at me. Pleez, Lawd, pleez!" prayed Boudreaux fervently.

That very instant, the bear skidded to a halt, fell to his knees and clasped his paws together in prayer."

"Aaaaaw tank ya, Lawd!" said Boudreaux with a sigh of relief. "Tank ya!"

The bear began to pray out loud right at Boudreaux's feet: "Bless us o Lord and these thy gifts which we are about to receive..........!"

Answered Prayer

On The Safe Side

Boudreaux was in a serious car accident and wasn't going to pull through. Father June was called in to administer the last rites.

Whispering firmly, Father June said, "Denounce the devil, Boudreaux! Let him know how little you think of him and his evil!"

Boudreaux said nothing.

Father June continued, "Let the devil know that you reject him and all of his empty promises, Boudreaux!"

Boudreaux was still silent.

"Oh Boudreaux, why do you refuse to denounce the devil and his evil," asked Father June.

"Look Fadda," answered Boudreaux, "Til ah kno' ware ahm heddin', ah ain't goin' aggravate nobody, me."

Something Extra

Boudreaux died and was met by St. Peter at the Pearly Gates. "I know you," said St. Peter. "You're Boudreaux, the Cajun. You were a pretty good guy on earth and didn't cause a lot of trouble. For that, I want to offer a gift to you of one special thing you've always wanted."

"Cot dawg! Das real nice o' you, yeah, Pete," said Boudreaux. "Tellya wat, ah always wanted, me, one o' dem lazy-boy reclining chaairs dere. Someting, dere, dat ah could jis sit back, relax and not worry bot nuttin'."

"That's an easy wish. Granted!" said St. Peter. "You'll have that chair as soon as you enter the Gates."

Next, a group of nutria appeared.

"Ah remember you," remarked St. Peter. "You were such good nutrias on earth. You did no harm to anyone and never hurt any other animals. Therefore, I want to grant you one special wish you've always wanted."

The chief nutria replied, "Well, we always watched the children playing and saw them roller skate. It was beautiful and looked like so much fun. So can we each have some roller skates, please?"

"Granted," said St. Peter. "You shall have your wish."

The next day St. Peter is making his rounds inside the Gates and he sees Boudreaux.

"Well, Boudreaux, did you enjoy the lazy-boy recliner chair?" asked St. Peter.

"Haaaaaw yeah!" responded Boudreaux. "Ah sho luv dat chaair me. By da way, Pete, dat "Meals on Wheels" ting, dere, wuz a real nice touch, too, yeah!"

Heavenly Question

Boudreaux died and was met by St. Peter at the Pearly Gates. St. Peter told him he could enter heaven only if he could answer one question.

"Dat ain't gon be no prablum, Pete," said Boudreaux. "Go ahed and axe me."

"Who sang the theme song for the movie 'Titanic'?" asked St. Peter.

"Cot dawg, das so easy, dat!" exclaimed Boudreaux. "Dat wuz dat cute lil ting from Canada, dere, uh uh uh Saline Dionne."

"That's correct," replied St. Peter. "Come on in. Look, Boudreaux, I need your help. I've got some business to take care of so would you watch the Gates for me for a few minutes?"

"Sheeeee, ahd be glad ta do dat faw you, me," answered Boudreaux. "Beside, ah ain't got nuttin' else ta do, das faw sho."

In the meantime, Shawee, Cowan and Chlotilde all appear at the Pearly Gates and are excited to see Boudreaux there.

"May wat happened ta yall?" asked Boudreaux.

"We wuz in a caw wreck, us, and we din make it," replied Shawee.

"Well, da ting is, ahm watchin' dese Gates, dere, faw Pete and yall kin only come in if you kin each ansa a question," explained Boudreaux.

"May okay, if das da way it work," said Shawee.

"Shawee, you go furst, you," said Boudreaux. "Wat wuz da neem o' da ship dat wreck inta da iceberg? Dey jis made a movie abot it, dere."

"Chooooo! Das as easy as eatin' some franch bread!" exclaimed Shawee. "Dat wuz da Titanic."

Boudreaux let him through the Gate.

Boudreaux turned to Cowan and decided to make the question a little harder. "How many people died on dat ship?" questioned Boudreaux.

Fortunately for Cowan, he had just seen the movie and answered, "Abot fifteen hundred."

"Das rat," said Boudreaux, "You kin come in, too."

Boudreaux then turned to Chlotilde and said, "Okay, beb, na neem dem!"

Cajun Ten Commandments

Boudreaux and Shawee were having a cup of Community coffee one morning and became engaged in conversation.

"May how's Junya doin' in skool, him, Boudreaux?" asked Shawee.

"Ta tel da troot, not too bad," replied Boudreaux. "But he's havin' him a lil bit o' trouble in catechism class, dere."

"Wat kinna trouble?" questioned Shawee.

"He got a lil prablum wit da Tan Camanments," explained Boudreaux. "He can't remamba all dem high falutin' words, him."

"So watchu gon do?" inquired Shawee.

"Ah jis tol'm ta put dem in arryday Anglish, me. Dat way it gon be eazy fo'm," said Boudreaux. "So ah hep him out by writin'em so he kin undastan dem."

"Aw yeah? Ya got a copy witchu?" asked Shawee.

"Dere you go," said Boudreaux pulling a sheet of paper out of his pocket. "Ah tink he kin remamba dis, me. Lemme read'em faw ya.

1. Dey ain't got but one God, non.
2. Don't be cussin' at God, and nobody else faw dat matta.
3. Be sho ya go ta church arry Sunday, you.
4. All da time lissen ta ya mama and ya poppa, yeah.
5. May sha, don't kill nobody, non.
6. Be sho ya don't sleep wit yo fran's ole lady.
7. Don'tcha be stealin' nuttin' from nobody, you.
8. Tol da troot all da time abotcha neighba.
9. Don't be wantin' ta pass yosef a good time witcha neighba's wife.
10. Don't even tink abot ya neighba's pirogue or crawfish nets, dere."

"Sha lawd, Boudreaux, das so eazy even ah kin remamba dem," said Shawee.

"May me, too," said Boudreaux. "Na if ah kin jis folla dem!"

Let's Make A Deal

When Boudreaux was a little boy, he went to his mother demanding a new bicycle. She decided that he should take a look at himself and the way he behaved.

"Well Junya," she said, "It ain't Christmas, sha, and we ain't got da money faw no new bike. Why don'tcha jis wrat a letta ta Jesus and pray faw one instead?"

Junya didn't like her answer and threw a temper tantrum. His mother sent him to his room. He finally decided to sit down and write a letter to Jesus.

"Deer Jesus,
Ah been a good boy dis year, me, and would sho lika new
bicycle.
Yo fran,
Junya Boudreaux"

Now Junya knew that Jesus really knew what kind of boy he was, a real brat. So he ripped up the letter and decided to give it another try.

"Deer Jesus,
Ah been an okay lil boy dis year, and ah want me a new bike.
Yours truly,
Junya Boudreaux"

Junya knew this wasn't totally honest so he tore it up and tried again.

"Deer Jesus,
Ah tought abot bein' good dis year, so kin ah hava bike, me?"
Junya"

Well, Junya looked deep down in his heart, which is what his mother really wanted him to do. He knew he had been terrible and was not deserving of anything. He crumpled up the letter, threw it in the trash can and went running outside. He aimlessly wandered about depressed because of the way he treated his parents and his poor behavior. He finally found himself in front of a Catholic church. Junya went inside, knelt down and began looking around not knowing what he should do.

Junya finally got up and began to walk out the door. As he was walking, he was looking at all the statues. All of a sudden he grabbed one and ran out the door. He went home, hid it under his bed and wrote this letter:

"Jesus,
Ah gotcha mama, me. If ya aver wanna see hur agin',
gimme dat bike!"

Spiritual Food For Thought

Boudreaux and Cowan were kicking back with a few Buds at a back yard bar-be-que.

"Ya kno, ah been tinkin' a lot abot relijun lately, me," confessed Cowan.

"How come?" asked Boudreaux.

"Oh, ah don't kno," said Cowan. "Ah guess it's jis cuz da olda ah git, dere, da closa ah kno ahm gittin' ta meetin' da Big Guy upstairs."

"Huh, das faw sho," replied Boudreaux. "But wat kinna tings ya been tinkin' abot, you?"

"Like how come wen we talk ta God dey call it prayer, but wen God talk back dey call it schizophrenia?"

"Ah can't ansa dat, me," said Boudreaux. "Ta tell da troot, ah din even kno, me, dat schiz, ur schizo or watava da heck ya call it, dere, had annyting ta do wit God."

"And dey say dat probly on da atheist's tombstone gon be dis: 'Here lies an atheist, all dressed up and nowares ta go.'"

"Sha lawd, dat gon git yo attantion, yeah!" said Boudreaux sipping his Bud. "Wat else you tink abot, you?"

"Uuuuuh, dat da Bible tell us ta luv our neighba and ta luv our anemies, too," said Cowan.

"Aw yeah, das cuz dey probly da seem people!" commented Boudreaux.

"And den it say in da Bible dat da lion and da lamb gon lay down tagetta, dem," continued Cowan.

"Maybe so, but ah kin garontee you one ting, sha, da lamb ain't gon sleep much, non!" remarked Boudreaux. "Cot dawg, Cowan, ah sho liked ya a hol lot betta wen you tought abot nuttin' but da rolla derby, yeah!

Surprise! Surprise!

As Kymon passed by Boudreaux's house, he noticed him sitting on the front porch looking very depressed. He stopped in to see what was bothering his "podna."

"Cot dawggit, Boudreaux, ya sho look down, you," remarked Kymon. "May wat's da matta?"

"Me and Chlotilde done got inta a big knock-down-drag-out fight, dere," explained Boudreaux. "And ah feel bad, bad abot it, me."

"Aw yeah? "commented Kymon. "Watchall wuz fightin' abot?"

"Aw, ah jis tole hur a joke abot da Pope," answered Boudreaux.

"You couyon, yeah!" responded Kymon. "Ya kno Chlotilde's Catlic, hur."

"Haw yeah! But ah din kno da Pope wuz!" explained Boudreaux.

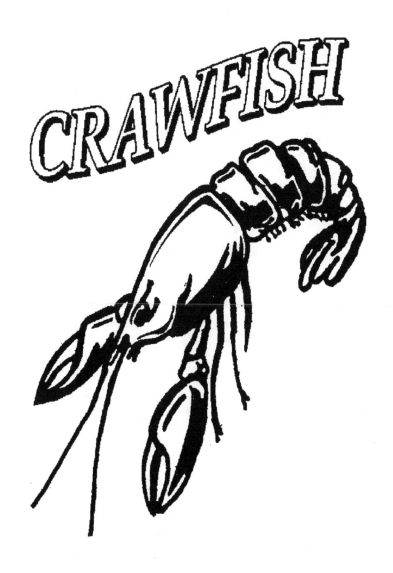

You just might be a Cajun if.....

You played your first game of Bourre while sitting in a high chair.

Your outboard motor has more horsepower than your car.

Some words you'll probably
never hear a Cajun say.....

"Da huntin' season oughta be a lil shorta, yeah."

"Cot dawg! Da New Orlin Saints is in da Supa Bowl!"

Chapter 11

Boudreaux On Sports & Recreation

Memory Loss

"How wuz ya gulf geem taday, beb?" inquired Chlotilde.

"Ah hit da ball purty good but ah don't see so good no mo', me," replied Boudreaux. "Ah can't tell ware it go wen ah hit it."

"May, watchu axpect? You saventy-five years old, you," said Chlotilde. "Why don'tcha take yo brudda, Pierre, witchu wen ya go?"

"Caaaaaw, he's eighty-five, him, and he don't even play gulf no mo'," said Boudreaux.

"Yabbut he got dat twanny-twanny vision, him," responded Chlotilde. "He got da perfect eyesight, and he could watch yo ball wen ya hit it."

Boudreaux took her advice and invited Pierre to accompany him to the golf course the next day. Pierre was watching intently as Boudreaux teed up the ball for his first shot. His swing was flawless and the ball disappeared done the middle of the fairway.

"You seen ware it went, you?" asked Boudreaux.

"Haw yeah!" yelled Pierre peering off into the distance.

"May jis don't stand dere, couyon, tell me ware it's at!" commanded Boudreaux.

"Ah fogot!" said Pierre.

The Winning Score

Boudreaux was watching a baseball game when Cowan stopped by for a visit.

"May wat's da score?" asked Cowan.

"Saven ta tan," answered Boudreaux.

"Who's winnin'?" questioned Cowan.

"Da tan," said Boudreaux nonchalantly.

Salty To The Last Drop

Boudreaux and Shawee went fishing behind Golden Meadow. They were in Shawee's boat and weren't catching anything, so they decided to head home. As they were coming in, they met T-Boy who had two ice chests filled with fish. Naturally, they wanted to know where he caught them.

"May ware you caught all dem fish, you?" asked Boudreaux.

"Jis go out dat pass ova dere til da wata git fresh," instructed T-Boy. "Stop dere and jis drop ya line."

With excitement and anticipation, Shawee steered the boat toward the pass. When they got a little ways out, Shawee told Boudreaux to fill a bucket with water and taste it.

Boudreaux did as he was told and replied, "Cot dawg, Shawee, dis wata still is salty."

Shawee went further out and told Boudreaux to taste the water again. Once more Boudreaux did as he was told and responded, "Pooyie, it's still salty, yeah!"

They continued in the pass for another hour and it was starting to get dark. They were in the middle of nowhere and weren't sure exactly where they were. Shawee told Boudreaux to quickly taste the water one last time.

"But Shawee, dey ain't got no mo' wata in da bucket!" exclaimed Boudreaux.

Fishy Story

Boudreaux called home from work one Monday morning. "Oh beb, someting jis came up, dere. Ah got me dis chance ta go fishin' faw da whole week," said Boudreaux. "It's da oppachunity o' a lifetime! We goin' leave rat away, so how bot you pack my clothes, my fishin' equipment, and faw sho' my blue silk pajamas. Ahm goin' be home in abot an hour ta pick'em up."

Boudreaux hurried home, grabbed everything Chlotilde had packed and rushed off. He returned a week later.

"You had yosef a good trip, you?" asked Chlotilde sarcastically.

"Haw yeah! It was good, good, good!" answered Boudreaux. "Da only ting wrong wuz you fogot ta pack my blue silk pajamas." "Aw non ah didn't!" shouted Chlotilde angrily. "Ah put'em in ya tackle box!"

Priorities

A man won a free ticket to the Super Bowl from his company for being the top salesman. Unfortunately, when he arrived at the stadium, he realized that his seat is in the last row of the top section. He was closer to the Goodyear blimp than he was to the field.

Halfway through the first quarter he noticed an empty seat ten rows off the field right on the fifty yard line. He decided to take a chance and made his way through the stadium and around the security guards to the empty seat. As he sat down, he asked the gentleman sitting next to him, Boudreaux, "Excuse me, sir. Is anyone sitting here?"

"Aw non," replied Boudreaux, "Dere ain't nobody dere."

Now, very excited to be in such a great seat for the game, he again inquired of Boudreaux, "This is incredible! Who in their right mind would have a seat like this at the Super Bowl and not use it?"

"Well, ta tellya da troot," said Boudreaux, "Dat seat belong ta me. Ah wuz supposed ta come wit my wife, Chlotilde, but she pass away, hur. Dis is da furst Supa Bowl dat we ain't been tagetta since we wuz married in 1967."

"Well, I'm very sorry to hear that and know how sad you must be," said the gentleman. "But still, couldn't you have found someone to take the seat? A relative or close friend maybe?"

"Maaaaay non, dey all at da funral, dem," explained Boudreaux.

Sports Minded

Ole Boudreaux was a very hard worker and spent many of his nights bowling or playing volleyball. One weekend, Chlotilde decided that he needed to relax a little and take a break from sports, so she took him to a strip club.

The doorman at the club spotted them and said, "Hey Boudreaux! How are you tonight?"

Chlotilde was quite surprised and asked, "May beb, you been here befo'?"

"Aw non, sha," answered Boudreaux. "Das jis one o' da guys ah bowl wit."

They were seated and the waitress approached, sees Boudreaux and said, "Nice to see you, Boudreaux. A Budweiser as usual?"

Chlotilde's eyes widened and she asked in an annoyed tone, "You mus come here a lot, you, huh?"

"Ah guess not!" replied Boudreaux indignantly. "Ah jis kno hur from volleyball, me!"

Then a stripper walked up to the table, threw her arms around Boudreaux and asked, "A table dance as usual, Boudreaux?"

Chlotilde was fuming at this point. She collected her things and stormed out of the club. Boudreaux followed her and spotted her getting into a cab so he jumped into the passenger seat. Chlotilde looked at him, seething with fury and anger, and began her tirade.

At this point the cabby leaned over and said, "Sure looks like you picked up a real live wire tonight, Boudreaux!"

Killing Two Birds With One Stone

The room was full of expectant mothers and their husbands, and the Lamaze class was in full swing. Boudreaux and Chlotilde were in that number. The instructor was teaching the women how to breathe properly, along with informing the men how to give the necessary assurances at this stage of the plan.

The teacher then announced, "Ladies, exercise is good for you. Walking is especially beneficial. And gentlemen, it wouldn't hurt you to take the time to go walking with your wife!"

The room became very quiet. Finally, Boudreaux raised his hand.

"Yes, Mr. Boudreaux," said the instructor.

"Hey teach, you tink it'd be alrat, dere, if Chlotilde carried da gulf clubs while we walk?" asked Boudreaux.

You just might be a Cajun if.....

You use two or more pirogues to protect your tomato plants from a late frost.

You ask, "You still working by Mitch, you?"

Some words you'll probably never hear a Cajun say.....

"Dey sho ain't got enuff cookin' shows on da talavision set, non."

"Ahm goin' be glad, me, wen dey got computas arrywares."

Chapter 12

Boudreaux On Technology

Short Wave Radio

Shawee stopped in to visit with Boudreaux one evening after supper. They were sitting at the kitchen table when Shawee spotted a brand new radio on the shelf.

"Cot dawg, looka dat nice lookin' radio, dere!" said Shawee. "Wen ya got dat?"

"Bot two week ago at da hawdware sto. Got me a real good deal, yeah!" said Boudreaux.

"May watchu waitin' faw, you. Go hed and put dat ting on so we kin ketch da Zephyrs baseball geem." instructed Shawee.

"Ah can't do dat, sha, cuz it only play in da mornin'," answered Boudreaux.

"Watchu mean it only play in da mornin'?" asked a puzzled Shawee.

"Maaaaay, it's a AM radio, couyon!" explained Boudreaux.

Pure Magic

Boudreaux was walking through the aisles at Wal-Mart when he approached the hardware section. The clerk told him that they were having a sale on thermos bottles.

"May wat dey do dem termos bottles?" asked Boudreaux.

"Well," said the clerk, "They can keep things very hot and also very cold."

He continued to expound on all of the advantages of having such an item. So Boudreaux decided to buy one.

At the lunch break at work the next day, Boudreaux and Cowan sat next to each other to eat. Naturally, Boudreaux pulled out the thermos bottle from his lunch kit and was proudly showing it off.

"May wat's dat?" asked a puzzled Cowan.

"Dat's a termos bottle," replied Boudreaux.

"Wat it do?" inquired Cowan.

Said Boudreaux, "It keep tings hot, hot, hot and cold, cold, cold."

"Chooooo, dat sound real good, yeah!" exclaimed Shawee. "Watchu got in dere?"

"Maaaaay, teree rasberry popsicles and a cup o' community coffee!" answered Boudreaux.

Flying High

Kymon decided to take sky diving lessons. He was taught that after jumping out of the airplane, he was to pull the ripcord to open the parachute. If for some reason that didn't work, he was instructed to pull the emergency cord. Soon after attending the lectures faithfully, the fateful day for his first jump arrived. The plane rose to an altitude of twenty-five thousand feet. The time had come. Kymon cautiously walked toward the open door, paused, then jumped. After free-falling awhile, he pulled the cord. Nothing happened. He quickly pulled the emergency cord. Still nothing. At this point he was in a state of panic and began frantically flapping his arms to slow his plunge. As he was falling, he looked down to see how far he was from the ground. Still very high, he couldn't believe his eyes. He saw Boudreaux on his way up.

"Hey Boudreaux," shouted Kymon wildly, "You kno anyting abot dem parashoots, you?"

"Haw, non," responded Boudreaux. "How bot you? You kno someting abot butane burners?"

Earning Your Wings

Shawee was the pilot for a routine cargo flight for Cajun Airlines. He asked Boudreaux to come along for the ride and to keep him company. One-half hour into the flight, the plane encountered some extremely turbulent weather and was bounced around viciously. Shawee hit his head on the steering mechanism and was knocked unconscious. The plane began drifting aimlessly so Boudreaux had to act fast. Not knowing anything about flying, he decided to try to make radio contact with someone.

He began shouting into the radio, "May day! May day! Dis is Boudreaux on da Cajun Arrline Flight #102.   Da pilot, dere, Shawee, done got hissef knocked out and ah don't kno nutting bot flyin' dis arrpleen, me! Ah need some hep quick, quick!"

"This is the control tower," came the response. "Don't worry, we'll walk you through everything and get you back on the ground safe and sound."

"Go hed, sha, ahm ready, me!" replied Boudreaux anxiously.

"First, how high are you and what's your position?" asked the voice from the tower.

"Maaaaay, ahm abot five foot tan and ahm all da way in da front o' da pleen," said Boudreaux.

"No, no!" answered the tower. "What's your attitude and where's your location?"

"Huh, ah kin tellya ah got me a real po' attitude rat na, yeah, and ahm from Cut Off, me!" replied Boudreaux.

"No, no, no!" came an exasperated voice. "I need to know how many feet you got off the ground and what's your plane's relation to the airport."

"May, countin' me and Shawee we got us fo' feet off da ground and ta tell da troot, ah don't tink dis pleen's related ta da arrport atall!" responded Boudreaux.

After a long pause, the tower came on and said, "We just need one more piece of information from you.........we need to know who's your next of kin and where to send the flowers!"

Break It To Him Gently

Chlotilde walked into the house and said to Boudreaux, "Oh beb, ah got some good news, me, and some bad news faw you."

"Well den, go hed and gimme da good news furst," said Boudreaux.

"Da good news is dat dem arr bag in da caw, dere, dey work real good, yeah!" said Chlotilde.

"May okay," said Boudreaux. "So wat's da bad news?"

Under Parked

Chlotilde rushed into the house and informed Boudreaux, "Da cawbarada on da caw got wata in it, yeah."

"May why you say dat? You don't kno nuttin' abot caws, you!" said Boudreaux.

"Cuz ah jis pawked it in da bayou!" explained Chlotilde.

Sweet Deal

Boudreaux wanted to sell his truck for fifteen hundred dollars but because it had two hundred thousand miles on it, couldn't get any offers. T-Brud gave him some advice concerning how to make it more appealing.

"Look," said T-Brud, "As long as you got two hundred tousand miles on dat truck, ain't nobody in dere rat mind goin' buy it. Ahm tellin' ya. Watcha gotta do is roll back da odometer ta read fifty tousand miles."

Boudreaux took his advice, made the change and waited. Several days later T-Brud passed by and saw the truck was still in Boudreaux's yard.

"Cot dawg, Boudreaux," said T-Brud, "You mean ta tell me you din sell dat truck yet?"

"Aw non, ah jis decided ta keep it faw mysef, me," explained Boudreaux. "It only got fifty tousand miles on it!"

High Tech Laxative

Boudreaux was on his first airplane flight and wasn't very brave. The captain had just earned his wings, and this was his first flight as such, too. The plane soon reached a cruising altitude of thirty thousand feet. A half hour later, the plane hit an air pocket and immediately dropped a thousand feet. Through expert maneuvering, the captain was able to keep the plane under control, and it finally settled down with a loud bang. He was proud of his efforts. But the cabin was a mess with papers and food flying all around as well as with hysterical passengers. The young captain, however, had been trained to pacify the passengers in times of turbulent weather in order to keep them from being afraid.

So the captain addressed them saying, "Your attention, please. This is your captain speaking. Just checking. Did you see what I just did?

Then came a voice from in the back of the plane which said, "Dis is passenja Boudreaux and you oughta come ova here and see wat ah jis did, me!"

No Computer Whiz

MAMO

To: Da boss
From: Ya new employee - Boudreaux
Abot: Dis Y ta K ting

Ah jis hope, me, dat ah din misundastan ya instructions, cuz, ta tellya da troot, none o' dis Y ta K radot make anny sanse ta me, non.

Annyhow, ah did watchu axed me ta do. Ah jis finished chengin' ova all da munts on my calenda so dat da year two tousand is reddy ta go wit da followin' new munts and days:

Januark, Februark, Mak, Julk

Mondak, Chewsdak Wednesdak, Tursdak, Fridak, Saturdak, Sundak.

Makes Sense To Me

Boudreaux and T-Brud were engaged in their favorite pastime, having a few brews at the Hubba Hubba.

"Oh Boudreaux," said T-Brud, "Ah heard, me, dat ya wuz scaid ta fly in one o' dem arrpleens. Fo' true?"

"Haw yeah!" replied Boudreaux as he sipped his beer.

"May how come?" inquired T-Brud.

"Cuz da las time ah got on one dem arrpleens, me, it hit one o' dem arr pocket, one o' dem pothole in da sky you kno, and dat pleen drop abot a tousand feet in no time atall," explained Boudreaux. "Cooooot dawg, ah tought ah wuz a goner, me. Ah wuz so scaid dat ah almos ruined me a good, good pare o' conson, yeah!"

"May you tink you goin' aver fly agin, you?" questioned T-Brud.

"Huh, only if dey start makin' dem pleens outa da seem kinna stuff dat dey make da lil black box out of dat hold da cockpit recorda!" responded Boudreaux as he gulped the rest of his beer.

Deadly Discovery

Chlotilde and Boudreaux went to the hospital to have their baby delivered. Upon arrival, Doctor Fontenot informed them that he had invented a new machine that would transfer a portion of the mother's labor pain to the father.

He asked, "Would you folks be willing to try this new procedure?"

"Haw yeah!" exclaimed Boudreaux. "Annyting das goin' hep Chlotilde wit da laba peens ahm goin' do, me!"

"Sha, you so sweet, you!" said Chlotilde affectionately.

Doctor Fontenot set the pain transfer at ten percent for starters, explaining that even ten percent was probably more pain than the father had ever experienced before.

But as the labor progressed, Boudreaux felt fine and said, "Go hed and pop dat macheen up a few mo' notches dere, dock. Ah feel good, me!"

Doctor Fontenot adjusted the machine up to twenty percent pain transfer. Boudreaux was still feeling fine. The doctor checked Boudreaux's blood pressure and was amazed at how well he was doing.

"Ahma tuff son-a-ba-gun, me!" exclaimed Boudreaux proudly. "You kin crank it up sumo, yeah, dock!"

Doctor Fontenot decided to try fifty percent. Boudreaux continued to feel very good. Since the pain transfer was obviously helping out Chlotilde considerably, Boudreaux said, "Dock, go hed, dere, and gimme all da peen." And so he did.

Chlotilde delivered a healthy baby with virtually no pain. She and Boudreaux were thrilled and overjoyed.

When they got home, they found the mailman dead on the front porch.

Unsolved Mystery

Taxing down the tarmac, the jetliner abruptly stopped, turned around and returned to the gate. After an hour-long wait, it finally departed.

Boudreaux, a passenger on the flight, was very concerned about the delay. Since he had a strong fear of flying, his imagination ran wild with possible reasons for the inconvenience.

"Wat wuz da prablum, dere, Cap?" asked Boudreaux nervously as the steward passed by.

"It wasn't much," replied the steward. "The pilot was bothered by a noise he heard in the engine."

"May yall fixed dat ting, huh?" asked Boudreaux. "Das how come we had da delay, rat?"

"Not really," said the steward. "It just took awhile to find a new pilot."

In The Fast Lane

After years of playing the Louisiana Lottery, Cowan finally hit the jackpot. The payoff was two million dollars and he couldn't wait to start spending it. He quickly decided to buy a 1999 Ferrari GTO, one of the best and most expensive cars in the world, costing about $500,000. He test drove it and while stopped for a red light, Boudreaux pulled alongside him on a four wheeler. Boudreaux looked over the sleek, shiny surface of the new car and asked, "Sha, lawd, wat kinna caw ya got dere, Cowan?"

Cowan replied smugly, "It's a 1999 Ferrari GTO and it cos abot a half a million dolla."

"Cooooot dawg, das a lota money faw a caw, huh!" exclaimed Boudreaux. "How come dey cos so much?"

"Cuz dis lil puppy kin do upta teree hundred and twanny mile an hour, dere!" he answered proudly.

"May, kin ah see on da inside, me?" asked Boudreaux.

"May yeah," replied Cowan obligingly.

Boudreaux poked his head inside the window, looked around and remarked, "Chooooo, dis is a real nice caw faw sho, yeah!"

Just then the light changed and Cowan decided to show Boudreaux just what his $500,000 car could do. He floored it and within thirty seconds the speedometer read three hundred twenty mph. Suddenly, he noticed a dot in his rear view mirror. It seemed to be drawing closer! He slowed down to see what it could be and suddenly, whoooooosh! Something whipped by him, going much faster!

"Wat da heck dat could be goin' fasta dan my Ferrari?" Cowan asked himself. Then, ahead of him, he saw a dot coming toward him. Whooooooh! It went by him again, headed in the opposite direction. It almost looked like ole Boudreaux who was on the four wheeler.

"Haw non, dat can't be," thought Cowan. "How could a fo'wheela outrun my Ferrari?"

Again, he saw a dot in his rear view mirror! Whoooooooh! Kabooooom! This time, it plowed in the back of his car, demolishing the rear of the Ferrari. Cowan leaped out of his car and saw that it was ole Boudreaux who had just been admiring his vehicle. Of course Boudreaux and his four wheeler were in poor shape. He ran up to Boudreaux and said, "Pooooo Boudreaux! You hurt bad, yeah! Wat kin ah do ta hep ya?"

"Well, ta start wit," moaned Boudreaux. "You kin unhook my suspanders, dere, from yo side view mirra!"

The Cajun Night Before Y2K

Boudreaux and Shawee were guzzling Budweisers at the Hubba Hubba, making plans for the new year and the new millennium.

"How you keem tarew dat Y2K prablum, you, Boudreaux?" asked Shawee.

"Cooooot dawg! Dat wuz da mos scairest nite o' my life, me!" exclaimed Boudreaux.

"May watchu meen?" probed Shawee.

"Well, lemme 'spleen it ta ya dis way," began Boudreaux.

"'Twuz da nite befo' Y2K
and all tarew da nation,
we waited faw Da Bug
da millennium sensation.

Da chips wuz replaced
in computas wit care,
in hopes dat ole Bugsy
wouldn't stop dere.

While some folks could tink
dey wuz snug in dere beds,
uddas had visions
o' dread in dere heds.

And Chlotilde wit her PC
and me wit my Mac,
had jis log on da Net
and kicked back wit a snack.

Wen ova da serva
dere rose such a clatta,
ah called Mista Gates, me,
ta see wat wuz da matta.

But he wuz away
so ah flew lika flash,
off ta my bank
ta witdraw all my cash.

Wen wit my wanderin' eyes
should ah see,
my good old Mac
sho' look sick ta me.

Da hack o' all hackas
wuz lookin' so smug,
Ah knew, me, dat it must be
Da Y2K Bug!

His image downloaded
in no time atall,
he whistled and shouted
let all systems fall.

Go Intel, go Gateway
now HP and Big Blue,
Arryting Compaq
and Pentium, too!

All processors dat are big
and doze dat are small,
crash away, crash away,
crash away all!

All da controls
dat pleens need faw dere flights,
all microwaves, treens
and all traffic lights.

As ah drew in my breat
and wuz turnin' aroun',
out tarew da modem
he came wit a bound.

He wuz covered wit fur
and slung on his back,
wuz a sackful o' virus
set faw da attack.

His eyes how dey twinkled
his dimples how merry,
as midnight approached
tings sho' got real scairy.

He hada broad lil face, him,
and a roun' lil belly,
and his sack filled wit virus
shook like some jelly.

He wuz chubby and plump
all da time grinnin',
and ah laff, me, wen ah saw him
dough my hard drive stopped spinning.

A wink o' his eye
and a twist o' his hed,
Soon gave me ta kno
a new feelin' o' dread.

He spoke not a word
but went straight ta his work,
He chenged all da clocks
Den turn wit a jerk.

Wit a twitch o' his nose
and a quick lil wink,
all tings elactronic
soon went on da blink.

He zoomed from da system
ta da next folks on line,
he caused so much disruption
could dis be a sign?

Den ah heard him axclaim
wit a loud, hearty shout,
happy Y2K ta ya all
dis is one hellava nite!"

"Na, ya see wat ah meen, you?" asked Boudreaux. "Hey Cap,
bring us sumo brews ova here in a hurry, sha!"

Fully Loaded

Boudreaux was driving a Yugo and pulled up at a stoplight
next to a Rolls Royce. He rolled down his window and shouted to
the driver of the Rolls, "Hey, Cap, das a nice lookin' caw ya got
dere, sha. Ya got a talafoam in ya Rolls? Ah got me one in my
Yugo."
The driver of the rolls looked over and simply said, "Yes, I
have a telephone."
"All riiiiight!" said Boudreaux. "Hey, ya got a fridge in dere,
too? Ah got me a fridge in da back seat o' my Yugo!"
The driver of the Rolls, looking quite annoyed, said, "Yes, I
have a refrigerator."
"Cot dawg, das great!" beamed Boudreaux. "Hey, ya got
yosef a TV in dere, too? Cuz ah got me a TV in da back seat o'
my Yugo!"
The driver of the Rolls, extremely annoyed by now, said, "Of
course I have a television! A Rolls Royce is the finest luxury car
in the world!"
"Well ahm sho glad faw you, sha!" said Boudreaux. "Hey,
you got a bed in dere? Ah got me one in here!"
Upset that he didn't have a bed, the driver of the Rolls Royce
sped away. He went straight to the dealer where he promptly
ordered that a bed be installed in the back of his Rolls.

The next morning the driver of the Rolls picked up his car. The bed looked superb, complete with silk sheets and brass trim. It was clearly a bed fit for a Rolls Royce.

So the driver of the Rolls began searching for the Yugo. He looked all day but had no luck. Finally, late that night, he found the Yugo, parked with all the windows fogged up from the inside. The driver of the Rolls got out and knocked on the Yugo. When there wasn't an answer he knocked again and again. Eventually, Boudreaux stuck his head out, soaking wet.

"I now have a bed in the back of my Rolls Royce!" the driver of the Rolls stated arrogantly.

Boudreaux looked at him with disgust and said, "You got me out da showa faw dat?"

Cajun Technician

Boudreaux and T-Boy were downing a few cold ones at the Hubba Hubba and began discussing the advantages of having a computer.

"Dey good, yeah," said Boudreaux. "Da only bad ting, dough, is dat ya start ta depand on dem too much."

"Ga-lee!" exclaimed T-Boy. "Wat happen if it go out on ya?"

"Like annyting else, dere," explained Boudreaux, "Ya jis gotta call yosef a tachnishun. But dey ain't cheap, non, and dey kin be kinna messy!"

"Sha lawd, ah don't kno, me, if ah wanna fool wit all dat," said T-Boy.

"Ya jis gotta chenge wit da times, T-Boy," insisted Boudreaux. "You gotta git wit it. But annyhow, ah got dis here offa da innaneck da udda day, dere, and ah tought it wuz kinna funny, me. Lemme read it ta ya."

"Okay, but les git us annuda beer furst, dough," said T-Boy.

"Here we go, podna," said Boudreaux.

'Tan ways ta tell if a Cajun dun worked on yo computa:

10. Da monita is up on some blocks.

 9. Da outgoin' faxes got gumbo steens on'em.

8. Da six front keys, dey, got holes in'em.

7. Da xtra RAM slots got outboard mota parts stored in dem.

6. Da numba keypad only go up ta six.

5. Da password is 'sha'.

3. Dey got a Tabasco bottle in da CD-ROM drive.

2. Da keyboard, dere, is camouflaged.

AND, da numba one way ta tell if a Cajun, dere, been workin' on ya computa.....

1. Dey call da mouse a 'shawz'."

"Das funny alrat," laughed T-Boy. "But it ain't gon be my prablum, non, sha, cuz ah ain't gittin' no computa, me!"

You just might be a Cajun if.....

The women in your family can't dance until they take their shoes off.

Your family and friends are nicknamed after their favorite food, like "Pop Tart".

Some words you'll probably
never hear a Cajun say.....

"We ain't gotta worry bot no hurrikeens dis year, us."

"It git a lil hot here, yeah, but it's a dry heat, sha."

Chapter 13

Boudreaux On Work

Logical Deduction

Down around the Louisiana-Texas border, there had been a rash of illegal cock fighting and gambling. The Director of the Louisiana State Police finally bowed to public pressure and sent an investigator to solve the problem.

The crack investigator, Boudreaux, took an unmarked car and headed for DeRidder to crack the case. After three days of intensive investigation, he returned to Baton Rouge to report his findings to his boss.

"Well, what did you find out, Boudreaux?" asked the top cop.

"Dat dey got teree groups in cahoots in dis cock fightin' ting," replied a confident Boudreaux. "Dey got some o' dem Texas Aggies, some Cajuns, and da Mafia."

"That's an odd bunch," said the Director. "What evidence did you find to bring you to that conclusion?"

"Well," said Boudreaux, "Ah put on a disguise and went ta one o' dem fights ta see faw mysef. It come clear ta me rat away. Ah knew rat off da bat, me, dat some Aggies wuz involved wen somebody put a duck in da fight."

"What else?" asked the Director.

"Ah could see dey hadta have some Cajuns tangled up in dere somewares wen ah saw dat somebody bet on da duck."

"Well what brought you to the conclusion that the Mafia was involved?"

"Maaaaay, cuz da duck won!" exclaimed Boudreaux.

Close But No Cigar

Boudreaux applied for an engineering job in Shreveport in North Louisiana. A local man applied for the same job and both applicants, having the same qualifications, were asked to take a test by the department manager. Upon completion of the test, it was learned that each man had missed only one question.

The manager confronted Boudreaux and said, "Thank you for your interest, Boudreaux, but we've decided to give the job to the local man."

"How come ya gonna do dat?" asked a disappointed Boudreaux. "We made da seem score on da tes. We bote got forty-nine questions rat outa fifty!"

Explained the manager, "We based our decision, not on the correct answers, but on the one you both missed."

"And jis how da heck one wrong ansa kin be mo bedda den da udda?" asked a frustrated Boudreaux.

The manager replied, "Simple! The local put down on question #5, 'I don't know'. You put down 'me needa'!"

His Own Worst Enemy

Boudreaux, Shawee and Kymon were working on a new high rise in New Orleans. When completed, it was going to be the tallest building in the city. The threesome sat together for their lunch break everyday.

When Boudreaux opened his lunch box, he couldn't believe his eyes. "Tuna — tuna sandwich agin! Ahm sick o' dat tuna and mynez and ah can't take it no mo, me! If ah git tuna and mynez agin tamorra, dere, ahm goin' jump offa dis building, ah garontee ya!" promised Boudreaux.

When they broke for lunch the next day, Boudreaux slowly opened his lunch box and took out his sandwich. It was tuna and mayonnaise. True to his word, he jumped.

"How come he done someting so stoopid like dat?" asked Shawee.

"May watchu meen?" inquired Kymon.

"Maaaaay, cuz Boudreaux, him, he fix his own lunch arryday!" said Shawee.

The Whole Truth

"Oh Boudreaux, you aver heard from dat camical cumpny on da river, dere, ware you applied faw a job?" asked Shawee.

"Aw yeah, ah heard from dem alrat," said Boudreaux.

"May you got da job, you?" inquired Shawee.

"Haw non, dey tore up my application, dem," replied Boudreaux.

"Tore it up? May how come?" questioned Shawee.

"Cuz o' one o' my ansas," responded Boudreaux.

"Watchu meen?" asked Shawee.

"Well, dey axed faw my neem, talafoam numba, social security numba and udda work experiences, dere," explained Boudreaux. "Dat wuz no prablum. Den dere wuz dis blank ware dey axe abot sax. So me, ah tol'em da troot. Ah put down yeah — one time, in Opelousas. So dey sed dey din needa smart alec workin' dere!"

Flooding The Engine

Boudreaux was cutting the grass along the bayou behind his house. As he cut along the edge, the lawnmower slipped out of his hands and fell in the bayou. Shawee soon came by and saw his "podna", Boudreaux, looking very depressed sitting on the bank.

"Wat's da matta witchu?" asked Shawee.

"Aw, my brand new lawnmota slipped outa my hand, dere, and fell in da bayou," explained Boudreaux. "Ah don't kno how ahma git it out, me."

"May dat's not a prablum, dere," said Shawee. "Ah kin do dat faw ya."

And with that he took a deep breath and dived into the bayou. Shawee was under water for at least five minutes and still there was no sign of him. Boudreaux was getting worried so he stuck his head under water to try to locate him. Within seconds he could see Shawee repeatedly pulling the rope on the mower.

Boudreaux, shaking his head in disgust, yelled, "Couyon, ya gotta choke it furst!"

Nature's Viagra

Boudreaux was plowing the land behind his house with his mule. Shawee was walking by and noticed something very strange.

"May Boudreaux! You crazy, you?" asked Shawee. "How come you plow like dat wit no pants on?"

"Das Chlotilde's idear, hur," answered Boudreaux.

"Why in da world would she wancha ta do dat?" inquired Shawee.

"Cuz yestiddy ah plowed all day long wit no shirt, me, and las nite ah wound up wit a stiff neck," explained Boudreaux.

We Love To Fly And It Shows

Boudreaux got his first pilot's job with Delta Airlines flying a passenger plane out of New Orleans to Jamaica.

On his first flight as captain, he announced to the passengers, "Good mornin', arrybody. Dis is ya Captin, Boudreaux. Ah wanna tank yall faw takin' da chance wit me flyin' on my furst job wit Dalta Arrlines. Ah sho' hope it ain't goin' be my las one edda. Ah wish we have us a safe trip ta Jamaica. Rat na we at eight tousand feet in da arr, and we goin' clime ta twanny eight tousand feet befo' it's all ova. Cot dawg, das high, yeah! Ah jis wanchall ta kno dat yall in good hands and we got us a good, good arrpleen here. Dis is da pleen wit fo' engines. We plan on makin' it ta Jamaica in abot two hours, dere. So pleez jis unlax and enjoy da trip. Da waita, he goin' go aroun' in a lil while and serve yall some good Cajun coffee and some breakfast. Lata on, dere, da barmaid, she goin' go check witchall ta take ya drink orda. We all goin' pass oursefs a good time on dis trip, yeah!"

Twenty minutes into the flight, one of the left engines started burning.

Boudreaux announced, "Uuuuuh, dis is yo Captin, Boudreaux. Ah guess yall probly noticed dat one o' da engines on da lef side ain't workin' good atall. Don't worry yosef abot nuttin', non. Ah jis cut off da gas ta dat one and we okay, us. We got us teree mo' good engines ta make it ta Jamaica. So jis unlax cuz you in good hands wit Captin Boudreaux."

Thirty minutes later, one of the engines on the right side started smoking and burning.

Boudreaux announced, "Dis is yo Captin, Boudreaux, agin. Ah sho hope all yall is enjoying ya ride ta Jamaica. Yall mita noticed dat one o' da engines on da rat side o' da pleen ain't workin' so good, edda. Ahma tellya someting, me. It's sho hawd ta fine a good mechanic taday, yeah. But we still okay, us. Ah cut off da gas ta dat one, too, so don't worry abot a ting cuz we still got us enuff engines ta make it ta Jamaica. Wit two good engines lef, we in good shape, us. Jis keep unlaxin' cuz you in good hands wit Captin Boudreaux."

Fifteen minutes later, the second engine on the left side started smoking and burning.

Boudreaux announced, "Dis is still yo Captin Boudreaux. Ah sho hope yall enjoyed ya breakfast. Ah jis wanchall ta kno dat dat wuz some fresh boudin, yeah! Well, yall probly noticed by na dat da sacand engine on da lef side ain't workin' no mo. You kin kiss dat mammer jammer goodbye, yeah, sha. Annyhow, ya kin feel safe cuz ah jis turn off da gas ta dat one, too. But don't worry abot it, non, cuz we got us one mo good engine lef ta make it ta Jamaica and it ain't dat far away. It's jis abot dis far on da map. Unlax yosef cuz you in good hands wit Captin Boudreaux."

Ten minutes out of Jamaica, the last engine started smoking and burning.

Boudreaux announced, "Dis is yo Captin, Boudreaux, and da drinks is on da house! Boy, if we jis had us one mo' engine, us! Cot dawg! Ahm purty sho' yall noticed by na dat da las engine, dere, jis conked out, but don't worry abot it, non, cuz dis pleen kin glide and we goin' make us a safe emergency landin'. Ah got a lota axperience, me, makin' dem emergency landin's. Dis pleen kin make a soft, soft landin' on da wata. Ahm jis goin' land dis lil puppy bot fawty yards from da beach. Rat na, dough, ah want arrybody dat kin swam ta sit on da lef side o' da pleen and arrybody dat can't swam ta sit on da rat side. Wen ah land dis pleen in da wata abot fawty yards from da beach, da waita and da barmaid, dey goin' open da emergency doors on da lef. Wen dem doors open, dere, all doze sittin' on da lef dat kin swam, yall jump in da wata and swam ta da beach. All da ones dat can't swam, dere, ahd jis like ta tank yall faw choosin' Dalta!"

Reach Out And Touch

Boudreaux barely managed to graduate from law school and was finally able to hang out his shingle. He rented a small office and waited for the phone to ring. For weeks absolutely nothing happened. Then one day there was a knock on the door. He quickly sat in the chair behind his desk and picked up the telephone. He yelled for the person to come in.

Boudreaux began speaking on the phone as the man entered. "Look, sha, don't worry yosef abot nuttin', non. Ah done faced dis lawya a lota times befo', me, and ah done whip his behind arrytime. We goin' win dis big case wit no prablum atall. Jis putcha mind at ease, dere." And with that he hung up the phone, turned to the man and asked, "May wat kin ah do faw ya?"

"Nothing really," replied the man. "I'm with the telephone company and I'm am here to connect your phone."

One Hundred Percent Effort

Cowan caught up with Boudreaux at the Hubba Hubba where he was "drowning his sorrows."

"Oh Boudreaux, ah heard dat you los ya job, you," said Cowan. "Cot dawg, ahm sho sorry ta hear dat, me. May wat happened?"

"Ah don't kno, me," replied Boudreaux. "Ah gave dat job arryting ah had — one hundred persant — twalve persant on Monday, twanny-teree persant on Chewsday, fawty persant on Wednesday, twanny persant on Tursday and five persant on Friday. Ah jis don't kno wat mo dey want, dem."

Check and Recheck

Boudreaux reported to the Civil Service office to take a placement exam. The test consisted of all true/false type questions. He took his seat in the examination room and stared at the test paper for approximately five minutes. Then in a fit of inspiration, he reached in his pocket and pulled out a coin. He started tossing the coin in the air and marking the answer sheet — heads for true, tails for false. Within half an hour he was finished whereas all the others in the group were still testing.

During the last few minutes of the testing period, the exam coordinator saw him desperately throwing the coin in the air and swearing repeatedly.   He became alarmed and approached Boudreaux.   He asked, "Mr. Boudreaux, what in the world is going on?"

"Well, ta tel da troot," replied Boudreaux, "Ah finished dat tes, me, in only tirty minutes. But jis to be on da safe side, ahm goin' back and checkin' my ansas."

Have It Your Way

Boudreaux began "moonlighting" at a local motel, and it was his first night on the job. A customer walked in and said he wanted a room.

"Das gon be fifteen dolla a nite," explained Boudreaux. "But if ya make yo own bed, it only gon be five dolla a nite."

"Sounds good," said the guest, "I think I'll make my own bed."

"Den wait rat here," said Boudreaux, "Ahma go gitcha da nails and da wood."

A Hard Cut

Boudreaux was shopping for a saw to cut down some trees in his backyard. He went to the hardware store and asked about various chainsaws.

The salesman said, "Look, Boudreaux, I've got a lot of models to choose from, so why don't you save yourself a lot of time and aggravation and get the top-of-the-line model. This chainsaw will cut a hundred cords of wood for you in one day."

So Boudreaux took the chainsaw home with him and began working on his trees. After cutting for several hours and only managing to cut two cords of wood, he decided to quit for the day. "Ah kno wat ahma do, me," said Boudreaux to himself. "Ahma git up at da crack o' dawn tamorra mornin' and cut all da day long."

The next day he was up at dawn and cut and cut until nightfall. He managed to cut only five cords of wood.

"Dere's someting wrong wit dis cheensaw," thought Boudreaux. "Ahma take it back ta da hawdware sto, dere, and fine out wat's da matta wit it."

The salesman, baffled by Boudreaux's complaint, removed the chainsaw from its case. "Hummmmm," he said, "It looks fine to me."

Then the salesman started the chainsaw.

"May wat's dat noise, sha?" asked a startled Boudreaux.

Great Container

Boudreaux stopped by the local diner at noon, sat down at the counter and ordered a cup of Community coffee. The waitress, who was very busy, gave him his coffee and rushed off to help numerous other customers who were in need of service.

Boudreaux used both cream and sugar in his coffee and noticed that the sugar container was empty and there were no little packets of creamer in the rack. As the waitress rushed by, he asked her to bring him cream and sugar for his coffee. The waitress, busier than she could ever remember being before, rushed to the back to pick up more orders.

As she passed by the cabinet where the extra sugar and cream were kept, she sat the plate down and put sugar cubes in her bosom because both her hands were full. After she had served the two plates she was holding, she returned to Boudreaux and asked him, "How many sugar cubes did you want in your coffee, Boudreaux?"

"Two o' dem, beb," replied Boudreaux.

The waitress reached into her bra, pulled out two sugar cubes and dropped them into his cup. "And cream?" she asked.

Boudreaux looked her directly in the eye and said, "Ah dare ya, sha!"

Cajun Dinner

"Oh Boudreaux, how come ya got fired from yo job wit NASA?" asked Kymon.

"Cuz arrytime dey sed 'launch' ah lef and wenta git me someting ta eat, me," explained Boudreaux.

Lagniappe

Great food is a hallmark of Cajun country. It is reasonably safe to say that Cajuns enjoy cooking as much as they enjoy eating. These recipes are provided to whet your appetite and to broaden your cooking and eating experience. Enjoy yosef, sha!

Crab Dip

1 lb crabmeat
8 oz. Philadelphia cream cheese
1/2 cup green onions (chopped)
1 small clove garlic
1 tablespoon Tony Chachere's Creole Seasoning
1 package Hidden Valley Ranch Dip Mix
1 stick butter
   Tabasco & Worcestershire Sauce

Melt da butta and da creem cheese and den add all dem seasonings one by one. Dreen da crabmeat good, good and den add it ta da mixcha. Sha, ya kin frigerate dis or jis serve it in a Fondue pot. Das up ta you cuz ah ain't goin' tellya how ta serve it, me. But cot dawg, das good, yeah!

Southern Living Seafood Gumbo

3/4 cup vegetable oil
1 cup flour
2 onions (chopped)
4 ribs celery (chopped)
1 can whole tomatoes (chopped fine & undrained)
4 cloves garlic (chopped)
1/2 cup parsley sprigs (chopped)
1 teaspoon dry whole thyme leaves
1 teaspoon red pepper (Cayenne)
3 bay leaves
4 14 oz. cans chicken broth
2 lbs medium shrimp (peeled & deveined)
1 lb crabmeat
1 pint oysters (crab claws optional)
1 & 1/2 teaspoon salt
1/2 teaspoon black pepper

Furst ya maka roux. Heat da oil in a big pot or a dutch oven. You kno watchu got. Den add some flowa da whole time ya stirrin' while cookin' on a medium fiyuh faw tan ta fifteen minutes. Keep on stirrin', dere, til dat roux is da color o' a coppa panny. Na ya goin' put in da onyons and da salry and cook faw anudda tan minutes. Remamba, ya gotta stir arry na and den so it don't stick ta da bottom o' da pot and burn. Stir in da chicken brot, bring arryting ta a boil and cova. Cut back da heat a lil bit and simma faw tirty mo' minutes. Na ya goin' put in dem ersters and da crabmeat (claws, too, if ya usin'em) and simma faw anudda fifteen minutes dere. Rat na ya kin salt and peppa ta ya taste. Be sho ya don't fogit ta take out dem bay leafs, non. Ya kin garnish wit some parsley, some grated onyons, some chopped green onyons or some file'. You kno watchu like, sha. All das lef na is ta serve it ova some rice and gonflay yosef.

Broccoli Cheddar Crab Soup

1 block butter
1 large onion (chopped)
2 pints half and half cream
2 cans cream of mushroom soup
1 can water
1/2 jar cheese whiz
1/2 jar jalapeno cheese whiz
 1 pound crabmeat (preferably lump)
1 large fresh broccoli or 2 boxes frozen broccoli

Melt da butta, stir in da chopped onyon and saute til it's soft. Na put in da creem o' mushroom soup, da can o' wata, bote pints o' da haf and haf creem and simma faw abot tan minutes. Den ya add bote potions o' da cheese whiz and kinna let it melt down. Tarow in da crabmeat and let it simma faw anudda tan minutes. Mix in da broccoli and cook on a low fiyuh faw abot tirty ta fawty minutes. Na ya got yosef someting, dere, yeah, sha! Cooooot dawg!

Shrimp Jambalaya

1 teaspoon cooking oil
1 teaspoon flour
1 lb. shrimp (peeled & deveined)
1 onion (chopped)
3 cloves garlic (chopped)
1 medium sized bell pepper (chopped)
1 tablespoon parsley (finely chopped)
1 tablespoon Paprika
1 tablespoon Worcestershire Sauce
1 small can tomato paste
1 can whole tomatoes (chopped & undrained)
4 cups rice (white or wheat)

Heat da oil in da pot. Na put in da flowa and stir til it turn a
coppa panny color. Ya jis made yosef a roux, yeah! Cot dawg,
you good, you! Okay, na lowa da fiyuh and add da onyons, da bell
peppa, da salry and da garlic. Stir da whole time and den put in
ya shrimps. Saute' on a low fiyuh, dere, faw tan minutes. Drop
in da tamata paste and da whole chopped tamatas. Simma faw
anudda tan minutes, stir and add enuff wata ta cova arryting.
Cook all dis faw tirty minutes. Add da rice, ya stir it, and ya cova
it. Cook on a low heat, dere, faw twanny ta twanny-five minutes.
Keep it covered but no stirrin', non. Na ya kin eatcha hawt out, sha.

Seafood Stuffed Potato

For each serving use:

1 medium baking potato
1 tablespoon butter
1 tablespoon sour cream
1/8 cup chives (finely chopped)
1/4 cup crabmeat
1/4 cup boiled shrimp
1 slice cheese of your choice
1/4 cup mushrooms
1/2 tablespoon onion (finely chopped)
1/4 teaspoon garlic (finely chopped)
        lemon juice and Tabasco Sauce if desired

Prepair da patatas faw baking; wash and prick holes in dem. Na ya bake'm in da oven or da microwave. It don't make no matta, non. But if ya microwave dem, bake dem faw fifteen minutes on high. Let'em cool off and den cut'em in haf lentways. Scrape da patatas outa da skin and put'em in a bakin' dish. Na ya mash dem tatas and add da sour creem and da butta til melted. Easy, easy, ya fold (lil bit at a time) in da shrimps, da crabmeat, da mushrooms and da mash patatas inta skins (optional) or in a servin' dish. Top wit da cheese and da chives and place in a warm oven til da cheese dun melted. Ya kin garnish wit a few parsley flakes, bacon bits and jis a lil dash o' lemon juice and Tabasco if ya wanna. Das up ta you!

Crab Fricasse

1 cup flour (plain)
1 cup cooking oil
1 large onion (chopped)
6-8 fresh crabs (halved)
1 1/2 - 2 quarts water
   Salt
   Pepper

Make dat roux first, beb. Putcha flowa and oil in da pot on a medium fiyuh. Keep stirrin', and remamba, ya want da roux ta be da color o' dat coppa panny. Na ya goin' put da onyon in and saute' dat rascal. Once ya got dat dun, ya gon tarow in dem crab halves. Cooooot dawg, ah kin taste it alrady, me! Na add da wata and ya goin' cook it ta a tick consistency. Aroun' tirty minutes, dere, oughta be okay. Be sho ya sprinkle in some salt and peppa ta make it jis da way you like it, you. Sha, you kin even drop a lil Tony Chachere's Creole Seasoning in dere if ya wanna. Ah ain't gon tell nobody, me. Das upta you. You kno how you like it. Jis fix yosef some rice, dere, and ya reddy ta go. And you tink dat chicken, dere, is finga lickin' good? Shaaaaa lawd!

Headless Hog Head Cheese

1 Boston butt roast
4 large onions (chopped)
3 bay leaves
3 cloves garlic (minced)
1 tablespoon chicken base
3 envelopes Knox unflavored gelatin
   parsley (chopped)
   onion tops (chopped)
   salt and Cayenne Pepper to taste

Cut dat roast inta teree inch pieces. In a big pot, put ta boil da roast pieces, onyons, bay leaves, garlic, chicken base, salt, peppa and enuff wata ta cova teree inches ova da roast. Boil dat sucka til dat meat, dere, is tanda, tanda. (aroun' two and a haf ta teree hours) In da las tan minutes o' cookin', add da onyon tops and da parsley. Take it offa da heat and let it cool off in da pot til da meat kin be worked witcha hands. Break da meat inta lil bitty pieces. Na put in dat gelatin and mix good, good, good. Put arryting inta some aluminum pans and keep in da fridge overnite. Wen ya eat it is up ta you, yeah!

Apple Rabbit

1 rabbit (cleaned and cut into pieces)
2 large onions (chopped)
3 tablespoons cooking oil
1 tablespoon Italian Seasoning
2 cloves garlic (minced)
3 cups rabbit or chicken stock
2 tablespoons apple jelly
1 teaspoon mustard
    salt and pepper to taste

Brown dem onyons, sha, til dey golden brown. Add da garlic, da Italian Seasoning, and da rabbit. Brown dat rabbit. Add da stock and da res o' da ingredients. Cook til da rabbit is tanda, tanda. Add wata or stock as you need it. Serve ova some rice. Wit dis you kin feed abot eight reglar eatin' people, but only fo' Cajuns.

Crawfish & Andouille Sausage Cornbread Stuffing

1 pan prepared corn bread
1 pound crawfish (cooked)
1 lb. andouille sausage
1 medium onion (chopped)
1 stick butter
1/2 bell pepper (chopped)
2 ribs celery (chopped)
1 tsp. Italian Seasoning
1 tsp. A-1 Steak Sauce
1 tsp. Worcestershire Sauce
   salt & pepper to taste
1 cup seafood stock
1 capful liquid crab boil

Okay, here we go, sha. In da food processa, dere, medium chop da crawfish and da sausage. In one o' dem big saucepans, melt da butta and sweat da vegetibbles til dey clear. (make dem suckas sweat, sha) Na ya goin' add da crawfish and da sausage. Ya only cook dis faw five minutes, yeah. Add da Italian Seasoning, da A-1, da crab boil, da Worcestershire, and da salt and peppa. Na ya wanna crumble da corn bread inta da mixcha puttin' in da stock ta make it moist jis like ya want it. Dis stuffin' kin be used wit chicken, pork, quail, or anny kind o' roadkill dat you wanna try.

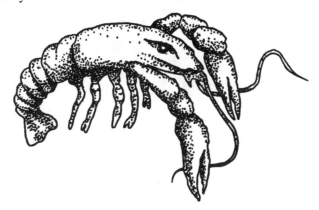

193

Quick Fixed Fish

6 pieces of fresh fish (your choice)
2 tablespoons margarine
  Seasonall Garlic Powder
  lemon pepper
  lemon Pam

    Take yosef abot six pieces o' nice size fresh fish. Season dem good, good wit da garlic powda and da lemon peppa. Spray bote sides o' da seasoned fish wit some lemon Pam. Na ya goin' spray da bottom o' da non-stick skillet wit some lemon Pam. (Ah wunda if she got a sista, hur?) Annyhow, brown da fish on a high fiyuh. Wen da fish is browned, dere, turn da fiyuh down low, low, low. Put in two tablespoons o' margarine and add a lil wata. Cova and let it steam til it's cooked. Ya kin spoon da juice ova some rice or some noodles. Ah sho ain't goin' telya wat ta do, me.

Roasted Wood Ducks

4 wood ducks cleaned but with skin left on (not da decoys, non!)
3 large onions (sliced)
1 bell pepper (chopped)
4 large potatoes (diced)
1 lb carrots (diced)
4 tablespoons oil
   McCormick's Seasoning Salt
   Accent
   lemon pepper
   Italian dressing
   Lee & Perrin Sauce

Okay, season da ducks wit McCormick's Seasoning Salt, Accent and da lemon peppa. Na ya marinate dem ducks in da Italian dressing and da Lee & Perrin Sauce in a covered dish. Put dat in da fridge faw two days, dere. (You ain't gotta stay and watch it, non You kin go somewares if ya want!) Put dem ducks in a magnalite pot wit fo' tablespoons o' oil. Cova da ducks wit da onyons and da bell peppa. Go hed and put it in da oven faw aroun' two hours, dere, at teree hundred and twanny-five degrees. Add some wata if ya got ta. Butcha bedda check dem doggone duck arry hour, yeah! Na take off da lid, dere, and tarow in da patatas and da carrots and put dat sucka rat back in da oven. Cook faw abot anudda hour and a haf, dere, wit da cova on da pot. Keep checkin' til ya kin see dat da vegetibbles are cooked and da ducks, dere, dey brown and tanda, tanda. Who you invite ta eat dem witchu is yo bidness, sha!

195

Pork Loin With Sweet Red Gravy

1 5 lb boneless pork loin
3 large onions (diced)
1 bell pepper (diced)
4 tablespoons flour
4 tablespoons sugar
4 tablespoons vegetable oil
1 can Rotel
1 cup mild picante sauce
1 can tomato sauce
1 cup Heinz ketchup
2 quarts water
  garlic
  McCormick's Seasoning Salt
  Accent
  Lemon peel from one large lemon

Sha, stuff dat poke loin wit garlic and season wit McCormick's Seasoning Salt, Accent, and some lemon peppa. Put in da fridge ova nite in a covered dish.

Brown da roast good, good ova a low fiyuh in aroun' fo' tablespoons of vegetibble oil. Wen dat roast is brown on all da sides, dere, add da onyons, da bell peppa and da lemon peel. Sha lawd, be sho ya use only da graded lemons, yeah! Wen da seasonings is brown, dere, put in fo' tablespoons of flowa. Brown dat flowa good, good.

Na ya goin' add one can o' Rotel. Pooooo, das goin' wake up yo taste buds fo' sho! Go hed an add da picante sauce, da tamata sauce and da ketchup. Got dat? Okay. Na bring arryting ta a boil and den let da roast and da ingredients cool off. Add abot two quarts o' wata and cook dat roast on a low fiyuh til it's tanda. And ah mean TANDA! Bot twanny minutes befo' da roast is finish cookin', tarow in fo' tablespoons o' shuga and stir real good. Fix yosef some rice and ya reddy ta go, beb!

Bread

6 cups Gold Medal flour
2 2/3 tablespoons sugar
2 2/3 teaspoons salt
2 packets Fleishmanns Yeast (1/4 oz. each packet)
2 cups warm water
1/2 cup dry (powdered) milk
1/2 cup oil

Da furst ting, dere, ya mix da yeast in two cups o' warm wata. Den ya mix all da dry ingredients (flowa, shuga, salt, milk) in a bowl and ya maka well (a hole) in da centa o' da bowl. Na add da oil and da wata/yeast mixcha inta da bowl and you knead it. Be sho you let it double in size. Chooooo! Abot an hour lata, knead dat dough down agin and let it rise. Put da dough in bakin' pans and, sha, let it rise, rise, rise. Na ya put dat mammer jammer in da oven and bake at fo' hundred degrees faw abot tan ta fifteen minutes. A lil tip. Git yosef some butta and spread it on da bread while it's still hot, hot, hot. Talk abot good, sha! Pooooo! Or mix yosef some peanut butta and surrup and dip dat bread in dere. Cot dawg, das someting, yeah!

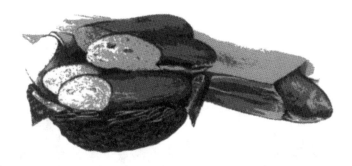

Persimmon Bread

3 eggs
2 cups sugar
1 cup oil
2 teaspoons salt
1 teaspoon baking soda
1 1/2 teaspoon baking powder
2 teaspoons vanilla
3 cups flour
2 cups persimmons (peeled & seeded)
1 cup pecans

Mix all dem ingredients tagetta and pour inta teree or fo' loaf pans. Bake at teree hundred degrees if ya use some dark pans or teree hundred and twanny-five degrees if ya use some light ones. Cot dawg, ya can't tell da difference, you? Den go axe ya neigh-ba. Annyhow, bake dem son-a-ba-guns faw fawty-five minutes, dere, and you all set, sha.

Bouille

1 12 oz. can pet milk (evaporated milk)
1 12 oz. can water
1 cup sugar
4 tablespoons corn starch
3 eggs
1 teaspoons vanilla extract
1 stick butter

    Warm da milk and da wata in a saucepan, dere. (But don't boil it, non) Blend da shuga and da cornstarch in a mixing bowl. Add dem eggs and den mix good, good, good. Na ya goin' add da egg mixcha ta da warm milk. Jis cook it til it tickens. Take it offa da heat and put in da butta and da vanilla. Stir dat ting, dere, til da butta is all da way melted. Ya got yosef someting na dat ya kin serve wit vanilla wafas, sheet cake or angel food cake. You got yosef eight ta tan servings, dere, sha.

COFFEE
&
BEIGNETS

Bread Pudding

10 slices bread
1 cup sugar
1 can evaporated milk (pet milk)
2 cups whole milk
1 teaspoon vanilla
4 egg yolks
1/3 cup butter or margarine (melted)
4 egg whites
1/4 cup sugar

Git yosef a nice mixing bowl, dere. Ya wanna break da bread up inta lil pieces and put in dat bowl. Na add one cup o' shuga, bote milks, da vanilla, dem egg yolks and dat melted butta. Take yo time and mix dem good, good. Dere ain't no reason ta be in no big hurry, non. Jis put arryting in one o' dem casserole (bakin') dishes and slap dat sucka in da oven. Bake dat ting at teree hundred and fifty degrees faw twanny ta twanny-five minutes. Den ya take it outa da oven.

Raise da tampachure o' da oven ta fo' hundred and fifty degrees. Na ya goin' make da meringue. Beat dem egg whites in a mixing bowl all da time adding one fort cup o' shuga, but slow, slow. Butcha only beat dis til ya git some soft peaks. Na, spread da meringue on top o' da puddin' in da baking dish and put it rat back in da oven. Be sho ya keep an eye on it, yeah, cuz ya gotta take it out wen da meringue turn light brown. Dis goin' cure yo sweet toot faw sho, sha!

Pecan Pralines

1 1/2 cups white sugar
  3/4 cup brown sugar
  1/2 stick of butter
  1/2 cup Pet milk (evaporated milk)
    1 teaspoon vanilla
    1 cup pecans (slightly chopped)
     waxed paper (freezer paper)

Put bote shugas and bote milks in a pot and mix dem up good, good, good. Put dat pot on a high fiyuh and cook til ya git ta da "soft ball" stage. Tarow in da butta. Wen dat butta dun melted, take da pot off da fiyuh and stir til da mixcha start ta ticken. Den ya put in da pacons and da vanilla and stir jis a lil bit til it's all mixed up. Ya shoulda alrady put yo wax paper on da table or counter and covered dat mammer jammer wit some butta. So na all ya gotta do is spoon it out on da wax paper and let it cool off. Dis goin' make abot twalve ta fifteen pralines, yeah. Lemme give ya a lil hint, sha. If ya candy start ta git hawd in da pot wen ya spooning it on ta da paper, jis add a few lil drop o' wata, dere, and stir it. Das goin' loosen it up faw ya in no time atall.

Squash Pie

1/3 cup sugar
1/4 cup corn starch
1/8 teaspoon salt
  2 large cans Pet (evaporated) milk
1/2 block margarine
  4 egg yolks
  1 teaspoon vanilla
  2 large handsfull shredded squash
     baked pie shell

     For the meringue
  4 egg whites
1/4 teaspoon cream of tartar
  8 tablespoons of sugar

Ya ready, sha. Okay, here we go, us. In a medium saucepan, dere, mix da shuga, da corn starch and da salt. A lil bit at a time, stir in da pet milk til it's smood, smood. Na cook dat sucka on a medium fiyuh til it tickens a lil. Slow, slow, ya stir some o' da hot mixcha inta da beaten egg yolks. Den ya goin' blend dis inta da res o' da hot mixcha in da saucepan. Zip in yo margarine and yo vanilla rat na. Jis cook til it tickens a lil bit. Ya ready ta tarow in ya shredded squash. Wat dis goin' do, sha, is lighten up da whole doggone mixcha. Butchu jis keep on cookin' and stirrin' all da time til it tickens. All ya gotta do na is pour it inta da baked pie shell.

Na make ya meringue, beb. Put dem egg whites and da cream o' tartar in a mixing bowl. Beat dat son-a-ba-gun while all da time ya puttin' in da shuga a lil bit at a time. Wen ya git dem soft peaks, dere, ya kno ya got ta stop beatin'.

Putcha meringue on da top o' ya pie and bake at fo' hundred degrees faw eight ta tan minutes, dere, or til it's done. Sha lawd, dis stuff kin knock ya socks off, yeah!

Summary

Volume II was just as much fun to put together as Volume I. The message is still the same — enjoy life, have fun, and continually look on the lighter side of things. You'll be doing yourself a tremendous favor if you do. Not only will you be healthier and happier, but certainly more pleasant to be around. It's your choice every single day. Choose to be happy and have fun as you carry out your daily responsibilities. Let ole Boudreaux be your guide.

Just in case you're wondering, yes, there will be a Volume III. But I can't do it alone. I need your help in acquiring stories, anecdotes, and other insights into the Cajun mindset and culture. Please feel free to send information to me via e-mail (curtboudreaux@cajunnet.com), fax (504-632-4898), or telephone (504-632-6177). I will gladly list you as a contributor in the next edition. I also invite you to visit my website: www.nolaspeaks.com/cb . I look forward to hearing from you. Until then, MAKE yourself a great day, sha, and may God bless!

Glossary

aaaaaw - aw exaggerated
abot - about
abotcha - about you.
Acadiana - the southwestern part of Louisiana, Lafayette and the
     surrounding area *
accidently - accidentally
achieva - achiever
afta - after
aftanoon - afternoon
agin - again
ah'll - I will
ah - I
ahda - I had
ahed - ahead
ahm - I'm
ahma - I am a, I am going
aligible - eligible
all da time - always *
all riiiiight - all right
alligata(s) - alligator, alligators
almos - almost
alrady - already
alrat - all right
andouille - a type of Cajun sausage used in gumbo *
anemies - enemies
anergy - energy
Anglish - English
annnnnd - and exaggerated *
anny - any
annyhow - anyhow
annymo' - anymore
annyting - anything
ansa - answer

* definition

ansas - answers
anudda - another
anvelop - envelop
anyting - anything
aroun' - around
arr - air
arrline - airline
arrpleen - airplane
arry - every
arrytime - everytime
arryware - everywhere
artritis - arthritis
asheem - ashame
askin' - asking
asprin - aspirin
assamble - assemble
at'em - at them
atall - at all
atcha - at your
attantion - attention
attractin' - attracting
aver - ever
aw - meaningless expression *
axacise - exercise
axam - exam
axcited - excited
axclaim - exclaim
axe - ask
axpect - expect
axpense - expense
axperience - experience
bad, bad - very bad *
bake'm - bake them
bakin' - baking
banket - banquet, sidewalk

* definition

barry - bury
batchla - bachelor
batta - better
battrum - bathroom
battry - battery
batween - between
bayou - a small body of water similar to a creek found in
     Louisiana and other parts of the southern United States
beb - baby, honey
bedda - better
befo' - before
behin' - behind
bein' - being
bestess - very best
betcha - bet you
bidness - business
bigga - bigger
birt - birth
birtday - birthday
bladda - bladder
bleeve'em - believe them
bleeve - believe
blend - to mix two or more ingredients until well combined *
blunk - blinked
boad - board
boat - both
bodda - bother
boddering - bothering
boodayed - to pout, be upset *
booksto - bookstore
borra - borrow
bot - about
bote - both

* definition

boucherie - a communal butchering of swine or cattle
    to ensure a fresh supply of meat and by-products
    for the participants*
boudin - (boo-dan) Cajun sausage *
Boudreaux - (boo' dro) n, (F), prolific Homo Sapiens attracted to
    swampy areas. Unhurried, unworried and prone to spells
    of procrastination *
bought'm - bought him
bouille - (boo-yee) - a vanilla pudding *
bourre - (boo-ray) a Cajun card game in which the loser of the
    hand must match the take of the winning hand*
breat - breadth
breen - brain
bress - breast
bringin' - bringing
bro - slang for brother *
brot - broth
brudda(s) - brother(s)
bullit - bullet
bumpa sticka - bumper sticker
buncha - bunch of
butcha - but you
butcha - butcher
butchu - but you
butta - butter
caaaaaw - slang used to express excitement or amazement,
    like chooooo *
cahoots - conspiracy, conspiring *
Cajun - a Louisianian who descends from French-speaking
    Acadians. Also one from several ethnic groups over which
    the Acadian culture prevailed.*
calenda - calendar
caliba - caliber
Camanments - Commandments
camical - chemical

* definition

can'tcha - can't you
cap - short for captain, used in lieu of someone's name *
captin - captain
captol - capitol
carryin' - carrying
cass - cast
Catlic - Catholic
caught'm - caught him
caw - car
cawbarada - carburetor
centa - center
chaairs - chairs
charry - cherry
chase'm - chase him
chasin' - chasing
checkin' - checking
cheensaw - chainsaw
chenge - change
chenged - changed
chengin' - changing
Chewsday - Tuesday
chiren - children
chockayed - incoherently drunk *
cholestrol - cholesterol
chooooo - slang used to express excitement or amazement
    (like caaaaaw) *
choosin' - choosing
clatta - clatter
clime - climb
closa - closer
cold, cold, cold - extremely cold *
comin' - coming
computas - computers
confusin' - confusing
conson - underwear, drawers*

* definition

contrack - contract
coooot dawg - cot dawg exaggerated *
coooot dawggit - same as cot dawg *
coppa - copper
coss- cost
cot dawg - expression like golly or gee *
coulda - could have
couldja - could you
couldna - could not have
countin'
coupla - couple of
couyon - crazy *
cova - cover
Cowan - French for turtle *
creem - cream
creen - crane
crossin' - crossing
cumpnies - companies
cumpny - company
curtins - curtains
cussin' - cussing, cursing
cut'em - cut them
Cut Off - a small bayou community in South Louisiana *
cuz - because
da - the
da paper - newspaper
daid - dead
dair - their
daire - dare
Dalta - Delta
dan - than
dannis - dentist
das - that's
dat - that
datcha - that you

* definition

datsa - that is a
daughta - daughter
dawg - dog
de - the
deat - death, debt
Deat Valley - Death Valley, LSU's Tiger Stadium *
decidin' - deciding
deenger - danger
deer - dear
deliva - deliver
dem - them
den - then
depand - depend
deprassed - depressed
deprassors - depressors
dere - there, their
dese - these
dey - they
dice - to cut food into cubes the shape of dice, usually about
    1/8 inch in size *
didja - did you
diffrence - difference
diggin' - digging
din- didn't
dinna - dinner
dirty rice - a Cajun dish made with rice and various kinds of
meats* dis - this
Dixie beer - local beer brewed in New Orleans *
dock - doctor
dockarhea - diarrhea
dockta - doctor
doggone - nice way of saying dam *
dolla - dollar
don'tcha - don't you
dough - though

* definition

doya - do you
doze - those
dreen - drain
dressin' - dressing
drinka - drinder
drinkin' - drinking
driva - driver
drivin' - driving
drunka - drunker
duck - duct
dum - dumb
dun - done
eatcha - eat your
eatin' - eating
eazy - easy
edda - either
eemed - aimed
eggstra - extra
elaction - election
elactronic - electronic
elavan - eleven
'em - them
embarrassin' - embarrassing
ennnnnh - an expression used instead of saying "what" or "eh" *
enta - enter
enuff - enough
eryster(s) - oyster(s)
etouffee - (a-too-fay) - the ultimate cajun dish usually made with
    seafood (shrimp or
evantually - eventually
fac - fact
Fadda - Father
faderal - federal

* definition

Fais-do-do - (fay-dough-dough) - a communal dance held
     traditionally in rural dance halls. Children were put to sleep
     at the dances giving rise to the term, fais-do-do, meaning
     "go to sleep" in Cajun French. *
famly - family
fareway - fairway
farma - farmer
fas - fast
fascinatin' - facinating
fasser - faster
fassest - fastest
fasta - faster
fava - favor
faw - for
fawty - forty
feelin's - feelings
feentin' - fainting
fellas - fellows
figa - figure
fightin' - fighting
filet knife - knife used to clean and filet fish
fine - find
finely - finally
fingas - fingers
fishaman - fisherman
fishin' - fishing
fix'm - fix him
fiyuh - fire
flashas - flashers
flowa - flour
flyin' - flying
fo' - for, four
fo'm - for him, for them
fogit - forget
fogive - forgive

* definition

fogot - forgot
fold - to blend a fragile mixture, such as beaten egg whites,
    delicately into a heavier mixture *
folla - follow
followin' - following
foteen - fourteen
foto - photo
frachured - fractured
fran(s) - friend, friends
franch - french
freeza - freezer
freezin' - freezing
fricasse - (frick-a-say) - a stew made from a roux *
fridge - refrigerator
frigerate - refrigerate
fucha - future
furst - first
ga-lee - golly, expression of astonishment
garontee - guarantee
geeeeet ouuuuut - get out (exaggerated)
geem - game
gimme - give me
git'm - get him
git - get
gitcha - get you
gittin' - getting
give'm - give him
gon - going to
gonflayed - full, stuffed *
gonna - going to
got'em - got them
got hitched up - married *
gotcha - got you
gotta - got to
govment - government

* definition

213

Grand Isle - small island community on the Louisiana coast *
gremas - (gre-mas' - roll the r) grimace, to make a face *
grinnin' - grinning
guarontee - guarantee
gulf - golf
gumbo - soup-like mixture made with a roux and several types
    of meats or seafood and served over rice *
guttin' - gutting
haaaaaw - slang term used for emphasis *
hackas - hackers
hadta - had to
haf-neckid - half-necked
haf-pas - half-past
hafa - half of
haid - head
hallo - hello
hare - hair
harecut - haircut
haunt - shy, embarrassed
hava - have a
havta - have to
haw non - oh no *
hawd - hard
hawdware - hardware
hawt - heart
healt - health
hearin' - hearing
hed - head
heda - he would have
hedache - headache
hedded - headed
heddin' - heading
hedlites - headlights
heeda - he would have
hellava - hell of a

* definition

hep - help
hereafta - hereafter
hidin' - hidin'
high falutin' - high faluting - high and mighty, important *
high, high, high - extremely high *
hissef - himself
hit'm - hit him
hol - whole, hold
hold'm - hold him
hona - honor
honkin' - honking
hoss(es) - horse, horses
hot, hot, hot - extremely hot *
Hubba Hubba - a bar and cafe in Galliano owned and operated by
    the Cajun Ambassador, Emmanuel Toups (now closed) *
huggin' - hugging
hume - home
humemade - homemade
hunta(s) - hunter, hunters
huntin' - hunting
hur(s) - her, hers
hurrikeen - hurricane
hurtin' - hurting
husbun - husband
ice box - refrigerator
idear - idea
iiiiit's - it's exaggerated
in'em - in them
infernal - internal
Injuns - Indians
innaneck - internet
inta - into
invanted - invented
ironin' - ironing
iscream - ice cream

* definition

it'd - it would

jis - just

jumbalaya - jambalaya - a mixture of different meats, seafood
    or poultry and vegetables

jumpin' - jumping

Junya - (Jun YA') Junior

jurned - joined

kabooooom - a slang term used to express a hit *

keem - came

ketch - catch

kickin' - kicking

kin - can

kinna - kind of

kno - know

knowin'em - knowing them

Kymon - French for alligator *

laba - labor

laff - laugh

laig - leg

laigged - legged

Laissez Le Bon Temps Rouler - French meaning "let the good
    times roll" *

landin' - landing

las - last

lata - later

lawnmotor - lawnmower

lawya - lawyer

leafs - leaves

leavin' - leaving

lectricity - electricity

lef - left

lemme - let me

Lent - a forty day period of fasting from Ash Wednedsay until
    Easter Sunday *

lentways - lengthways

* definition

les - let's
let'em - let them
letal - lethal
letcha - let you
letta(s) - letter, letters
lettus - let us
lika - like a
lil - little
lil bitty - very small
lissen - listen
lite - light
livin' - living
loafs - loaves
lobsta - lobster
looka - look at
lookin' - looking
los - lost
lost bread - French toast *
lota - lot of
lowa - lower
luv - love
luva - lover
luved - loved
maaaaay - may exaggerated
macheen - machine
macrow - ladies man *
maka - make a
makin' - making
mammer jammer - an expression used in the place of something
    else, often times something off color *
mamo - memo
mans - men
mantion - mention
Maree - (ma-ree' - roll the r), Marie

* definition

marinate - to soak in French dressing, vinegar, lemon juice,
    sour cream, etc.
Mass - Catholic worhsip service *
mat - math
matta - matter
maw maw - grandmother
Mawgret - Margaret
meen - mean
meentime - meantime
meetin' - meeting
ment - meant
merci beaucoup - French meaning "thank you very much" *
milkin' - milking
mirra - mirror
missus - a wife *
Mista - Mister
misundastan - misunderstand
misundastood - misunderstood
mita - might have
mite - might
mixcha - mixture
Mon Dieux - French meaning "my God" *
monita - monitor
Monsignor - title given to certain dignitaries in the Catholic
church *
mornin' - morning
mos - most
mota - motor
mota hume - motor home
mout - mouth
movin' - moving
mucha - much you
mud-'n-law - mother-in-law
munt - month
munts - months

* definition

murda - murder
mus - must
musta - must have
mynez - mayonnaise
mysef - myself
na - now
naaaaa - now exagerated, used in frustration *
nan-nan - nanny, nickname for Godmother *
Natchitoches - a small town in northwest Louisiana *
nava - never
neckked - naked
necs - necks
needa - need to, neither
neem - name
neems - names
neighba - neighbor
New Orlins - New Orleans
nite - night
non - no
nonk - uncle
nowares - nowhere
numba - number
nuttin' - nothing
o' - of
offa - off of
offen - often
offrin' - offering
okeration - operation
olda - older
ole - old
on'em - on them
onyons - onions
oppachunity - opportunity
orda - order
oughta - ought to

* definition

oursefs - ourselves
outa - out of
outgoin' - outgoing
outhouse - outdoor toilet *
ova - over
pacons - pecans
paleece - police
paleeceman - policeman
palican - pelican
pancil - pencil
panny - penny
parashoots - parachutes
pardnas - partners
pare - pair, pear
parrain - nickname for Godfather *
passenja - passenger
patata(s) - potato, potatoes
pawk - park
pawpaw - grandpa, grandfather
peen(s) - pain, pains
peenful - painful
peenkiller - painkiller
peent - paint
peppa - pepper
persant - percent
perscription - prescription
pet milk - evaporated milk
Phideaux - a Cajun spelling of fido *
pirogue - a small Cajun-style boat similar to a canoe *
pitcha - picture
planny - plenty
pleen - plane, plain
pleez - please
po' - poor
podnas - (pod NAS') partners, friends, buddies *

* definition

Point Au Chien - small community in southern Terrebonne
Parish in Louisiana *
poka - poker
poke - pork
pooooo - an expression used to emphasize a point *
pooyie - (poo-yii) offensive, taste bad*
popla - popular
poppa - daddy
poss - post
potata - potato
potions - portions
powa - power
powda - powder
prablum - problem
pragnant - pregnant
preciate - appreciate
prepair - prepare
pretand - pretend
prevantive - preventive
probly - probably
processa - processor
pucka - pucker
puddin' - pudding
purty - pretty
pushin' - pushing
put'm - put him
putcha - put you, put your
puttin' - putting
quarta - quarter
quick, quick - very fast, immediately *
racipe - recipe
radda - rather
radot - (ra-daught - roll the r) - mess, a disturbance *
ramote - remote
rast - rest

* definition

rat - right
ravenue - revenue
read'em - read them
recorda - recorder
reddy - ready
reen - rain
relijun - religion
remamba - remember
restrunts - restaurants
road - Rhodes
rolla - roller
roosta - rooster
roun' - round
roux - a flour and oil base used to make gumbo and gravy *
sacand - second
Sadday - Saturday
safa - safer
salabrations - celebrations
salid - salad
salry - celery
sance - since
sand - send
sanse - sense
sansitive - sensitive
santence - sentence
saramony - ceremony
saute' - to cook in a small amount of hot oil usually in
    an open skillet *
saven - seven
saventy - seventy
sax - sex
scaid - scared
scairest - scariest
scairy - scary
scripcha - scripture

* definition

'scuse - excuse
sed - said
seem - same
sef - self
sentcha - sent you
serva - server
sez - says
sha - cher, term of endearment *
sha lawd - sha lord
shaaaaa - sha exaggerated
shad rig - a type of fishing tackle used to catch two at a time *
shair - share
Shawee - French for racoon *
shawz - a thing, used in the place of something that you
    can't think of the name
sheeeee - a term used for emphasis *
sheem - shame
sho - sure
shoot'm - shoot them
shoulda - should have
show'm - show him
showa - shower
shrimpin' - shrimping
shuga - sugar
simma - simmer, to cook in liquid that is kept just below
    the boiling point *
simpla - simpler
sista(s) - sister(s)
skolla - scholar
skool - school
smackin' - smacking
smart alec - smart elec, wise guy
smart, smart - very smart
smood, smood - very smooth
sno - snow

* definition

snoplow - snowplow
soft boil - when making candy, the mixture can be rolled
    into a soft ball *
soft, soft - very soft
 someting - something
somma - some of
son-a-ba-gun - son of a gun
sooooo - so exaggerated
Sot Lafooche - South Lafourche (the southern part of the civil
    parish of Lafourche in South Louisiana) *
spacial - special
spacks - specks, speckled trout
spand - spend
spant - spent
speedin' - speeding
spittin' - spitting
'spleen - explain
stan' - stand
standin' - standing
stapping - stepping
stayin' - staying
stealin' - stealing
steens - stains
stinkin' - stinking
stirrin' - stirring
sto - store
stoopid - stupid
stop'em - stop them
stop'm - stop him
strawbarry - strawberry
strenge - strange
stuffin' - stuffing
sucka - sucker
suckin' - sucking
suga - sugar

* definition

sumo - some more
Supa - Super
suppa - supper
surrup - syrup
suspanders - suspenders
swam - swim
sweepin' - sweeping
swellin' - swelling
swig - sip *
ta - to
Tabasco - a pepper sauce used to spice up many recipes in
    south Louisiana and around the world
tachnishun - technician
taday - today
tagetta - together
takin' - taking
talafoam - telephone
talavision - television
talkin' - talking
tamata(s) - tomato, tomatoes
tamorra - tomorrow
tampachure - temperature
tampamantal - tempermental
tan - ten
tanda - tender
tangled up - involved *
tanite - tonight
tank - thank
tannnnnk - tank exaggerated
Tante - French for aunt *
tarow - throw
tarowing - throwing
tarown - thrown
tarrible - terrible
tatas - potatoes

* definition

taut - thought
teach'm - teach him
teems - teams
teet - teeth
tel - tell
tell'm - tell him
tellya - tell you
teree - three (roll the r)
termos - thermos
tes - test
tesses - tests
Texien - (Tex-e-en) a Texan *
Thibodaux - a small city in South Louisiana located in
      Lafourche Parish *
tickens - thickens
tickin' - ticking
tighs - thighs
til - until
ting - thing
tings - things
tink - think
tinkin' - thinking
tird - tird
tirty - thirty
tirty eight - thirty-eight
tol'em - told them
tol'm - told him
tol - told
tole - told
tolju - told you
tolme - told me
toot - tooth
tought(s) - thought, thoughts
tousand - thousand
traila - trailer

* definition

treened - trained
treenin' - training
treens - trains
trew - through
trippin' - tripping
troopa - trooper
troot - truth
trotlines - troutlines
trown - thrown
tryin' - trying
tuffa - tougher
tunk - thunk
turnin' - turning
Tursday - Thursday
twalve - twelve
twanny- fo' - twenty-four
twanny-twanny - twenty-twenty
twanties - twenties
'twuz - it was
udda - other
uddas - others
unda - under
undapaid - underpaid
undastan - understand
unfateful - unfaithful
unlax - relax
unlaxin' - relaxing
upta - upto
use'm - use him
usin'em - using them
usta - use to
uuuuuh - sound that indicates a hesitation or pause *
uuuuuh - uh exaggerated
vacuatin' - evacuating
vary - very

* definition

veens - veins
vegetibble - vegetable
vetrun - veteran
wafas - wafers
waita(s) - waiter, waiters
waitin' - waiting
wamans - women
wancha - want you
wanchall - want yall
wanchu - want you
wanderin' - wandering
wanna - want to
wantin' - wanting
ware - where
wares - where
waring - wearing
wat - what
wata - water
watava - whatever
watcha - what you, what your
watchall - what yall
watchu - what you
weeda - we would have
wen - when
wenaver - whenever
wenta - went to
wert - worth
wheela - wheeler
whetta - whether
whew - sigh of relief *
whooooo - a sound expressing excitement or exclamation *
whooooosh - swishing sound indicating something is passing *
winda - window
winnin' - winning
wit - with

* definition

witcha - with you
witchall - with yall
witchu - with you
witchu - with you
witdraw - withdraw
won - one
wooda - would have
woodja - would you
workin' - working
worsa - worser (worse)
worstest - the worse
woulda - would have
wrat - write
writin'em - writing them
wudn't - wasn't, was not
wunda - wonder
wundaful - wonderful
wundring - wondering
wuz - was
xtra - extra
Y2K - year two thousand, term given to the dilemma facing
    computers in recognizing double zero (00) as 2000 at the
    turn of the century.
ya - you or your
yabbut - yes but
yall - you all
yeah - yes
yestiddy - yesterday
yo - your
yors - yours
yosef - yourself
zackly - exactly
Zephyrs - New Orleans Triple A baseball team *

* definition

Bibliography

Bradshaw, Jim (Projects 2000 Editor). "Most Boudreaux
Families Arrived in 1785"
  Lafayette, LA, The Daily Advertiser, June 29, 1999.
  Adapted from: West, Robert. Atlas of Louisiana Surnames
  Reprinted with permission from Jim Bradshaw.

Conrad, Glenn (Editor). The Cajuns: Essays On Their History
And Culture.
  Lafayette, LA: Center For Louisiana Studies, 1978.

Woolfork, Doug (Publishing Editor). The Longest Street. Baton
Rouge, LA:
  Moran Publishing Corporation, 1980.

About The Author

Curt Boudreaux is a motivational speaker, author and Cajun humorist.   He received a B.S. degree from Nicholls State University in Thibodaux, Louisiana and a Masters +30 in Guidance and Counseling from Ole Miss.

In another life, he was an educator for twenty-four years and served as principal of Golden Meadow Middle School for ten. In 1988 he was honored as a National Distinguished Principal. This award is jointly sponsored by the United States Department of Education and the National Association of Elementary School Principals to recognize excellence in school administration. Only one public school principal from each state is selected annually for this award.

Curt is a member of the National Speakers Association and past president of the New Orleans Chapter.   He is also past Chairman of the Board of the South Lafourche Chamber of Commerce and past Chairman of the Board of Commissioners of Lady of the Sea Hospital.

He is a fourteen-year veteran of prison ministry work and is a volunteer in the Kairos Prison Ministry at Louisiana State Penitentiary at Angola.

Curt "retired" from education ten years ago to pursue a career in professional speaking.   He presents keynotes, seminars and workshops throughout the country addressing the topics of self-esteem, attitude, leadership and Cajun humor. You are invited to visit his web site at www.nolaspeaks.com/cb .

Curt works with individuals who want to improve the quality of their lives and with companies and organizations that want their people to develop their potential. His sense of humor, enthusiasm and passion for speaking combined with strong presentation skills enable him to relate easily to audiences and effectively communicate his message.

He is the author of *Never Kiss An Alligator On The Lips!* (Volume I) and *The ABC's of Self-Esteem.* He is also co-author of *Irresistible Leadership* and *Brothers Together.*

Curt has recorded two audio cassettes: "Never Kiss An Alligator On The Lips!" and "The Keys To Unlocking Your Potential."

Curt with his wife, Sue, and great-nephew, Derian, live in the small community of Cut Off, Louisiana, along the banks of Bayou Lafourche. This Cajun speaks from the heart! Let him speak to yours! Should you be interested in Curt speaking to your group or ordering products, you may contact him at:

Curt Boudreaux
Synergy Press
P.O. Box 422
Golden Meadow, Louisiana 70357

504-632-6177 - Telephone
504-632-4898 - Fax
curtboudreaux@cajunnet.com - E-mail
www.nolaspeaks.com/cb - Website

Programs

Never Kiss An Alligator On The Lips!
An entertaining talk, it centers on Cajun humor featuring the legendary stories of Boudreaux, the Cajun. It includes some "you just might be a Cajun if" thoughts and is ideal for banquets and after-dinner humor.

The ABC's of Self-Esteem
Attitude, belief in self, and confidence are discussed and their relation to building self-esteem. Participants are allowed to select areas of interest from the remaining twenty-three topic words. This talk corresponds to his book by the same title.

The Keys To Unlocking Your Potential
The focus of this program is to dream big dream, believe in yourself, and take positive risks. It is practical as well as inspirational and encourages participants to be all they can be. It coincides with his audio cassette.

The Human Side of Quality
This talk addresses improving the individual or employee through personal and interpersonal development as opposed to increasing his/her technical skills. The essence of self-esteem, human relations, and communication are examined and discussed.

You Only Go Around Once!
This inspirational talk is designed to encourage individuals to "go for it!" Rising above temporary defeat, being inspired, having courage and a zest for living are among the issues presented. It is laced with liberal doses of humor and is highly motivational.

The Art of Leadership
Effective leadership is crucial in many aspects of personal and professional life. Insights for improving leadership skills are viewed with an eye on qualities of a leader, leadership practices, myths and realities, and the leader versus the non-leader.

Winning Attitudes

As much as eighty-five percent of a person's success can be attributed to attitude. Participants come to grips with the importance of believing in oneself, having self-confidence, setting goals, and having high expectations. Possession of these attitudes can propel a person into the winner's circle.

Smart Discipline For Parents

This nationally acclaimed program is designed for parents with children of any age. The focus of this entertaining and innovative program is on discipline and self-esteem. Parents learn ways to stop fighting and bickering, gain cooperation and instill self-confidence in children.

Product Order Form

Never Kiss An Alligator On The Lips! - Volume I (Book)
Price: $20.00 (Louisiana residents add $1.50 sales tax per book)
Add postage/shipping costs at the rate of $2.00 for the first book and $1.00 for each additional book.

_____   Book(s) @ $20.00 + $1.50 tax per book .... _____

Postage/Shipping Costs . . . . _____

Never Kiss An Alligator On The Lips! - Volume II (Book)
Price: $20.00 (Louisiana residents add $1.50 sales tax per book)
Add postage/shipping costs at the rate of $2.00 for the first book and $1.00 for each additional book.

_____   Book(s) @ $20.00 + $1.50 tax per book .... _____

Postage/Shipping Costs . . . . _____

<u>**The ABC's of Self-Esteem: A Practical Approach**</u> (Book)
Price: $20.00 (Louisiana residents add $1.50 sales tax per book)
Add postage/shipping costs at the rate of $2.00 for the first book
and $1.00 for each additional book.

_____   Book(s) @ $20.00 + $1.50 tax per book . . . . _____

Postage/Shipping Costs . . . . _____

<u>**Irresistible Leadership**</u> (Book)
Price: $20.00 (Louisiana residents add $1.50 sales tax per book)
Add postage/shipping costs at the rate of $2.00 for the first book
and $1.00 for each additional book.

_____   Book(s) @ $20.00 + $1.50 tax per book . . . . _____

Postage/Shipping Costs . . . . _____

"Never Kiss An Alligator On The Lips!" (Audio tape)
Price: $10.00 (Louisiana residents add $.75 sales tax per tape)
Add postage/shipping costs at the rate of $1.00 for the first tape
and $.50 for each additional tape.

_____   Tape(s) @ $10.00 + $.75 tax per tape . . . . . . _____

Postage/Shipping Costs . . . . _____

"The Keys To Unlocking Your Potential" (Audio tape)
Price: $10.00 (Louisiana residents add $.75 sales tax per tape)
Add postage/shipping costs at the rate of $1.00 for the first tape
and $.50 for each additional tape.

_____   Tape(s) @ $10.00 + $.75 tax per tape . . . . . . _____

Postage/Shipping Costs . . . . _____

"The ABC's of Self-Esteem" (Poster) 18 X 24 four color
Price: $7.00 (Louisiana residents add $.50 sales tax per poster)
Add postage/shipping costs at the rate of $3.00 for the first 5 posters
and $.50 for every additional 5 posters.

_____ Poster(s) @ $7.00 + $.50 tax per poster . . . . _____

Postage/Shipping Costs . . . . _____

Total Amount Due . . . . _____

Make check or money order payable to
Curt Boudreaux and mail to:

Curt Boudreaux, P.O. Box 422, Golden Meadow, LA 70357

**Telephone (504-632-6177) * Fax (504-632-4898)
E-mail (curtboudreaux@cajunnet.com)
Website (www.nolaspeaks.com/cb)**

****

Name _____

Address _____

City _____

State _____ Zip _____

Telephone (_____) _____

****

_____ Please send details about Curt Boudreaux speaking
to my group.